Outcast

by Shimon Ballas

Outcast

by Shimon Ballas

translated from Hebrew by Ammiel Alcalay and Oz Shelach

City Lights Books
San Francisco

10 9 8 7 6 5 4 3 2 1

Cover design: Stefan Gutermuth
Text design and composition: Harvest Graphics

Editor: Robert Sharrard

Portions of this book have appeared in *Banipal, Beyond Baroque Magazine, Bombay Gin, Chain, Fascicle,* and *Words Without Borders.*

A Cataloging-in-Publication record has been established for this book by The Library of Congress

City lights Books are published at the City Lights Bookstore, 261 Columbus Avenue, San Francisco, CA 94133

Visit our website: www.citylights.com

To Gila

AFTER THE PRESIDENT SPOKE I got up to read the speech I had prepared but, to my surprise, I realized that I'd forgotten my reading glasses. I must have looked pretty confused up there, fumbling around through the pockets of my jacket and pants with the crowd staring and the television cameras all pointed at me. I was compelled to admit what had happened and the President broke out laughing, carrying the crowd along in a wave of applause, as if I'd just told a good joke. Butheina, sitting in the first row next to Hamida, was sending me all kinds of signals that, in my confusion, I couldn't interpret—I only later figured out that she was trying to let me know she could have read the speech instead of me. I never speak without a text in front of me and my heart races every time I'm called up on stage—and there I was, at a celebration in my honor at the Presidential palace and I found myself standing there naked and bare as the spotlights blinded me, making me look even more pitiful. I didn't remember even a single sentence of the speech I had written so I was left with no choice but to fold it up and put it back in my jacket pocket. I spoke for about ten minutes, and when I was done the President got up to shake my hand and give me a warm embrace. "We are all honored to have a man like you among us," he said. I stammeringly thanked him, too agitated to give him a proper response.

When all the speeches were over, Kazem had a look at the papers I had folded back into my pocket: "You spoke better, straight from the heart." Butheina also complimented me. The only reprimand I got, as usual, was from Hamida: "You see, just because you wanted me to go down to the car first, I couldn't keep an eye on you."

The ceremony was carried live on television and thousands of viewers saw me in my helplessness. Since then I've appeared on the screen a few times, on interviews and in discussions. I prepare myself very thoroughly before each appearance, asking to see the questions before we film, except the conversation never proceeds the way we plan and I'm forced to improvise my responses. Since retiring, I hadn't faced that kind of pressure and I've found it difficult, at my age, to get used to the draconian laws of television, to answer quickly and to the point without any possibility of revising or reformulating my thoughts. I do fine on radio, reading my answers while the host usually sticks to the script of questions he lets me look over beforehand.

Thank goodness all the excitement has finally subsided and the book is moving along its way to the reader. The reviews have been good, sometimes even enthusiastic. But, as usual, most of the critics didn't bother reading to the end, satisfying themselves with excerpts from the introduction and quotes from the three forwards. The expanded forward by Professor Elias Mattar of Damascus University is the one most often quoted, especially those sections where he emphasizes and even reiterates that my whole life's journey—from childhood in al-Hila to my studies in America and my years of service as a civil engineer and head of the National Lands Administration—was but one uninterrupted and diligent stride towards the writing of *The Jews in History*. I have no real reason to oppose such an exposition of things, but I remain suspicious of the kind of curiosity shown by journalists who prefer latching onto such a theory to dig into my past rather than write about the book itself. I began to insist that inquiries about the book remain substantial and told everyone who wanted to interview me that my only condition was not to ask me any personal questions. Kazem also agreed to convey my sentiments to all the newspaper editors he knew because I insisted that I had my reasons. I told him that I would write about my past myself, since this book was a scholarly work, no different really except in subject matter from any of the other scholarly books I had published until now. But I didn't let him know that I intended to write my memoirs and describe, in my own words, the trajectory that Elias Mattar had alluded to in his forward.

EVEN THOUGH THE COMMOTION has subsided, I'm worn out. I haven't had a break for months, and every time the phone rings my hearts skips a beat. Of what worth is the character of a man who can't say no, who responds once and then again until he can no longer refuse anyone. It began with an invitation to the Lawyer's Association, then an invitation from the Engineers' Club, the Officers' Club, the Medical School, the Writers Union, the Journalists Union; I was even invited to private homes and I found it difficult to come up with excuses for fear of insulting my hosts. I had to prepare myself for each meeting, not to mention the stream of visitors who came to congratulate me and spend hours in idle conversation. Not only did Hamida not rebuff any of them, she went so far as to encourage those who would feel uneasy lest they not pay me their respects. Receiving guests gave her the opportunity to show off her intelligence as a hostess of unequalled stature, but it was impossible to stop her from voicing opinions on things she knew nothing about. I was most beset at how proud she was to describe the way she supervised me: "Really, I have to force

3

him out to eat or bathe, otherwise he just shuts himself up in his room, completely oblivious." And no matter how hard Butheina tried to restrain her with very clear hints or even outright pleas, she just kept at it. She also never forgot to repeat her claim that because of my introversion, guests stopped coming to see us on *kubul* day, the way we used to celebrate it. I don't know what kind of an impression she made on people who didn't know her—I only hoped such visits would be both the first and the last of their kind. I'm tired of it all, tired and fed up.

Now she's taken Sabry under her wing, as if everything's just perfect since he came back. As for me, I like his company, even though his extremism is something I never cared for. He's sharp, and handsome, a smooth talker who always manages to make an impression. I'm just sorry for Butheina. She does her best to act naturally, but I see how much it oppresses her. I told her: "Patience, my dear, you know how your mother is." I don't think she'll last. It particularly vexes her to see the girl cleave to her father, joyfully taking off with him in the car. And every time the girl comes back with a present, my heart breaks to see the expression on Butheina's face, an injured look just on the verge of breaking into tears.

I try my best not to get involved since it will just lead to endless arguments with Hamida, and any argument with her is a lost cause right from the start. All the time Sabry was abroad she never stopped complaining. Unreliable, irresponsible, all over the place, a womanizer who didn't give a damn about his daughter. "The girl is angry at him," she told me one day, "I was sitting with her to look at some pictures in the album, and every time she saw her father's picture she turned the page. She didn't want to look at him. She's angry at him." And when I told her there was no need to exaggerate, she came back with her usual rancor: "You're always on his side, defending him, supporting him instead of your daughter!" But the tables have turned since the day Sabry came back. Ringing him with affection, she bestowed upon him the feeling that he was in the very bosom of the family, that he could come and go whenever he pleased. And Sabry repaid her measure for measure. He called her "Mother," and kissed her hand like a faithful son. And Butheina suffered, watching Sarah happy in the company of her mother and Sabry, while she went off to her room, superfluous, unwanted.

I'm at a loss. There is no one closer to me than Butheina. She's smart and sees things as they are but it's all bottled up inside her— the very opposite of Sabry who has the knack of drawing attention to himself—she can sit for hours without even uttering a sound. It isn't easy for an educated, independent woman like her in the company of men. Maybe if she gave the appearance of being tougher, she could find some balance with Sabry. Her reticence and restraint afflict her, while Sabry has always been spoiled and assumed everyone was there to appease him. He was always claiming that he tried to understand her and that it was she who was uncooperative. The fact is, despite all the virtues and good qualities he may have possessed, Sabry, like most men in our society, just lacked a certain sense of respect towards women. He grew up in a family that gave him everything, surrounded by servants, freed of all worry, and until he went to London, he'd never had to fend for himself. It's hard to even blame him, but Butheina was the one who got hurt. Thirty-three years old, mother of a little girl—it wasn't easy, the way we lived, for a woman like that to find the right match.

I've got more than some reason to think it was partially my fault. I wasn't aware of the deterioration in their relationship, and in the last two years that I was busy writing my book, I paid no attention to Hamida's warnings and just withdrew into my room. I had hoped things would work themselves out—I mean, when didn't people get into conflicts? But I just didn't take it into consideration, even though when I went to London, and stayed with them for a week, I saw things weren't the way they should be. I tried to account for it because of the way they lived, in cramped quarters because of the baby, the pressures of studying, it was easier for me not to think of the danger. But Butheina never hid her concerns from me, even her letters gave me more than a hint of her exasperation. Sabry stayed out a lot, saying he didn't even have a quiet corner left in the place while she, who was so diligent writing her doctorate, had to carry the whole burden herself. I wanted to believe that they'd find a way to pull things together when they returned, but the exact opposite happened, and the split was unavoidable. "It's not very pretty for him, but I won't give up my work just to pander to his manly honor." She had no difficulty getting accepted in the history department while he, after not finishing his thesis and agreeing to complete it here, insisted on going back to London with her. I was on her side and tried to get him to stay but it was already too late, the obstacles couldn't be removed.

He was brilliant and talented but there was something infantile about him—he caught on fast but lit out after every spark. He started in mathematics, then moved on to history before finally getting stuck in psychology. He excelled in every field, but couldn't stick to one. Did he regret it now? He certainly gave that impression. He needed warmth, people worrying about him, and I have little doubt that had Butheina been just a little more conciliatory towards him, he would have made a loyal husband and a fine father. But she wasn't like that; she was stubborn, and her stubbornness was the secret of her success. They just didn't fit together. Sometimes, when we're talking, I hear her uncle's voice: not just his voice, but his very manner of speaking, the rigid movements of her head. It's true, I'm also stubborn, but I think I'm a little more flexible when considering others.

"One of the best and brightest of the revolutionary generation," is how Kazem presented her to the President, "a daughter faithful to her people in following the path of her father." Indeed, following in my path, she chose a profession I was precluded from practicing for so many years and, like me, she paid very dearly for her choice. Should this have pleased me?

HE CAUGHT MY ATTENTION from my very first day at the hotel. His thick mustache, sharp gaze and a voice through which the very particular accent of the middle Euphrates came through loud and clear. There weren't too many guests in the lobby at the time and those who were sat hushed, in their traditional garb, alert as they spoke to each other. I turned to the table by the door and sat down to write Jane a letter. After a while, still absorbed in my writing and trying to block out everything going on around me, I sensed the presence of someone behind me and when I raised my head I saw him look at me with a faint smile on his lips. He stood upright and the *sidara* pitched at a slant on his head lent his face an ironic expression. He greeted me with a slight nod and turned on his way out with the measured step of someone completely sure of himself.

The next day I encountered his sharp gaze over lunch in the hotel restaurant. There was something mysterious about him that both intrigued and repelled me at the same time. I tried to keep from turning toward him until I finished eating. I wasn't really in the mood to strike up an acquaintance since I was preparing to leave the hotel and head back to Baghdad the next day. I hadn't found any of the friends I'd studied with in the two years I spent in Beirut—the only person I found at home was the English professor, a sickly, lonely man who lived off his pension and whose conversation left my spirit broken. The weather didn't do much to cheer me up either—grey skies and a strong chilly wind swept through the streets. End of November, the waterfront desolate, and no tourists expected until mid-December, for Christmas and New Year's.

In the evening I sat in the lobby reading the paper when, out of the blue, I heard a familiar voice beside me: "Might his honor be from amongst our cousins?" I got up to shake his outstretched hand. "My name is Kazem Sheikh Sha'aban," he said, and when I introduced myself he said, "Your name is familiar to me, you're from al-Hila, aren't you?" He sat next to me and our conversation flowed on late into the night.

I'm not the kind of person that's easy to make friends with. I have a deep aversion to revealing myself that's gotten more extreme over the years. I never felt it growing up in al-Hila or even later, in Baghdad—I was always surrounded by friends that I shared everything with and from whom I had nothing to hide, just as they had nothing to hide from me. Neither did I lack friends during the two years I spent in Beirut at the American University, even though I had already begun to feel the awakening of some sense of foreignness. It wasn't easy getting used to their way of life, especially since I was coming from a more closed society that hadn't yet fully taken on the ways of the west. In America I felt completely alien, in the full sense of the term: in the lecture halls, in the cafeteria, at student parties, I not only found myself the only Iraqi, but I was also usually the only Arab. All of that left traces in my behavior and reinforced my ascetic tendency, but the deciding factor came later, with the family scandal when I came back from America.

I'll speak about all this in due time since, after all, that's why I'm writing these pages. At any rate, on that same evening at the end of November 1934, after my parting visit with Jane, I met Kazem, and he's remained my friend throughout these fifty years. He fascinated me, his agreeable nature and voice bearing the delights of bygone childhood, as he carried himself like a noble tribesman from al-Diwanniya. He was on a business trip for the grain company that his family owned and ready to talk freely about all the things that concerned us in those days, when Iraq stood at a crucial crossroads in her history after the death of King Faisal. We exchanged stories about the days of the revolt against the Turks, something he had taken an active part in, even having been wounded in one of the battles. I spoke to him of my work as a civil engineer and my years of study in America, but he sensed that I was keeping something from him and about a month later, during one of our meetings in Baghdad, he said to me: "I admire your sense of restraint, those aren't things that are easy to talk about." Rumors had come to him and he had tried to verify them—when the opportunity arose for him to get to know Assad Nissim, he heard from him what I'd kept hidden. "Excuse me for probing into your circumstances behind your back," he said, and added: "It was only because of my regard for you that I did it, you should know that I understand and I'll always be there if you need me."

That's Kazem, the only friend left me in my old age. While Qassem 'Abd al-Baqi has been exiled to a foreign land, the twists and turns of life separate me and Assad Nissim.

THERE IS NO ONE more qualified than me to point out the contradictions in *The Jews and History*, even though I stand behind every sentence in it. This might sound somewhat Machiavellian, but a book of history, through its very existence, has a mission to fulfill, and my book is no exception. Historical research is not an objective science like the natural sciences; it deals with people, and whoever deals with people can not free themselves from personal predilections. And what better example for a lack of objectivity could one provide than books on Jewish history? But how is one to respond to the obvious question that comes up—are they the only fabricators?

I've just come back from a meeting with students from the departments of History and Semitic Languages at the university and, I must admit, I just barely escaped a well-laid trap. It isn't at all easy to create a sense of trust with these students, and it almost seems like some of them just show up to demonstrate their expertise in harassing the lecturer. I'm referring to a small number, three or four all in all, dispersed among more than a hundred in the lecture hall, who force you to turn your attention to them and conduct some sort of a dialogue. The rest respond with nods and smiles, or else just maintain an impermeable expression of passivity or indifference. In every encounter with students, the communists and their like especially stand out, bristling at every explanation or explicitly defying them. The most aggravating thing is that they manage to infect the whole atmosphere and create tension not only through themselves but among everyone else as well. They're also the only ones who come prepared with questions, but they aren't really interested in the answers even though they present them politely before their professors. That's what one guy did to me when he came up with a conundrum that seemed logical enough, and perhaps it even was: if, according to scientific research we can readily dismiss the fabricated contention of the Jews that Abraham was a Jew and father of the Hebrew nation, how can we prove that he was a Muslim, as it is written in the Quran? How could I possibly answer such a question? Should I have told him that Abraham was neither a Muslim nor a Jew, if he even existed? Scientific honesty would compel one to answer in this manner, but are we in the field of refined sciences here or in the theater of struggle against a cunning and resourceful opponent?

Luckily enough for me someone had given me a pamphlet before the lecture put out by the Syrian branch of the Ba'ath Party's Bureau of Information which claimed, among other things, that in 1800 B.C. there were already Jewish tribes in Southern Iraq that had migrated from the Arabian peninsula and simply continued north and west until they arrived to the Land of Canaan. I couldn't believe my eyes. How did they come up with such drivel? Had they just slavishly copied Zionist propaganda whose sole purpose was to penetrate the consciousness of the world with the notion that Jews laid claim not only to Palestine but to all the Arab lands from the Euphrates to the Nile? I avoided the student's question and instead began attacking the authors of the pamphlet for disseminating enemy propaganda at the same time that they claimed to be cautioning us against it. I also spoke about our own public relations policies which relentlessly kept repeating the same hackneyed slogans without tackling the roots of the problem; the chairman gave his full consent and even added that my book would prevent such drastic mistakes in the future.

I'd like to believe that's how it will be, but I don't think one or even a dozen books can change anything. Only power can change things, and power isn't on our side. That's the truth. And in the meantime, we're all wrapped up in our petty struggles while someone digs their nails into their fellow's throat. Socialism, Marxism-

Leninism, Maoism, everyone has their holy book. And the young partake of every dish, no matter how spoiled, as long as it comes from someplace else! Sabry walked around London with the *Little Red Book* in his pocket and he found the answer to every question in it. The same with Zuhair. A refined young man, quite the opposite of the contentious and indefatigable Sabry, he always listened politely while never straying an iota from his opinions. Qassem nurtured the seeds of rebellion in him from an early age and when the time came he fell right into an earthly paradise of believers. And how could you possibly argue about anything with Qassem? Nothing budged him from his beliefs, despite all the disappointments and failures he continued prattling on about the role of the proletariat in the socialist revolution! Imprisonment, torture, he was always in and out—and now where is he? Some say he's in Prague, alone in his old age.

I did what I could. I fulfilled my obligation. Maybe more to myself than to my readers. In these pages I can be open and freely express whatever it is I wasn't able to say in my other books. We're in a period of transition, and at times like this, when things are unstable, it's impossible to be decisive and preferable to say things that can be halved and quartered, to mix wool and linen, to say things that aren't in your heart, or not say the things that are. That's how it is with *The Jews in History*. A book for a time of transition, an effort to crystallize a national consciousness based on authentic premises. A scholarly text, but one bearing a message. If it achieves its goal, I'll have earned my keep and won't have to defend myself before those accusing me of any lack of consistency, of saying things that can be interpreted ambivalently. Anyone setting out to fulfill a mission is obligated to bear the consequences.

I mulled all this over on our way back and it seemed like

Butheina joined me in my ruminations, even though she kept quiet until we got home: "You look tired," she said, "these meetings are tiring you out." She spoke in allusions. I'm sure she was also thinking of the letter from her professor. I made a mistake and there is nothing I can do about it except regret that I let myself be persuaded to consign the introduction to him. They pressured me into accepting the reader's report, and the Ministry of Information prepared a faithful translation of the introduction into English and French. They hoped, as I too had hoped, to get supportive responses that could be included in the forward but, other than Prof. Ernst Grassmok from Brazil, an old friend who sent a letter full of praise, no one responded with anything worth quoting. They either evaded it or politely thanked us for sending the introduction. Only her Jewish professor couldn't resist an insulting response. I'm well aware that you're an engineer, but I would advise you to study some history before you start writing it! And so on. He didn't even bother reading my biography since he would have realized that I had studied history when he was still a kid. It disturbed Butheina and she wanted to write something back to him, but I stopped her. I didn't want him to know she was my daughter. An important and well-respected scholar, considered a friend of the Arabs, while she was just beginning her academic career. I told her that if he knew who I was and knew something about my past, his comments would have been even more virulent. I made out like it didn't bother me, but I felt the affront scathe me to my very soul. She told me that she would tell him everything at their next meeting. I didn't answer. By the time they met, if ever, it wouldn't even matter any more. He gave her his opinion and she certainly wouldn't be able to disprove it. I'm also trying to figure out what she thinks about the book and what she thought today at the student meeting. You're tired, these meetings tire you out. She won't reveal what she thinks and I prefer not knowing.

"I REMEMBER YOUR ARTICLE regarding the holidays," Kazem told me the first time we met in Beirut. He was referring to an article I published in 1932, which roused the wrath of the Jews against me, those who benefited most from recognition of their many holidays in government ministries and commercial life. I told him that until I began working in the city of Baghdad's engineering administration I had given no thought to this peculiar phenomenon, unparalleled in any properly run country, that religious minorities such as Jews and Christians holding key positions in official institutions should be absent from work and bring it to a complete halt for the entire duration of their holidays. Kazem did not conceal his wonder at hearing the demand for these privileges to be canceled from a man like me, but immediately added: "I'm happy for the privilege to know you, your article was a remarkable deed of patriotism."

During our conversation, which lingered into the wee hours of the night, and on the following day as well, I managed again and again to arouse his wonder, which I took as a compliment. "We are used to hearing different things from those who return from the West," he said. "They go away to acquire an education and come back as missionaries for a materialistic culture, dismissing religion and tradition, looking down on their fellowmen, and walking among their people like strangers, whereas you talk with such passion about Islam and the values it embodies!" I told him that I had just as much appreciation for the culture of the West, from which we have a lot to learn, but I do not forget for a second that it isn't ours. I added that as a free man who doesn't consider himself belonging to any religion, nothing hindered me from praising Islam. Kazem laughed: "But I, as a devout Muslim, am indeed hindered. I'd be accused of degeneracy, of incitement, of subversion!" And when we were about to part he said: "We complement each other, I on the inside, and you on the outside say similar things. I wish there were more people like you!"

We were young, brimming with high ambition, and Iraq was at the beginning of its road to independence, in dire need of construction, of raising its beacon high among the nations. This meeting with Kazem encouraged me greatly—he uplifted my downtrodden spirit and, in talking with him, I realized how right I was to have decided not to stay in America. Wearied by two weeks of travel, I had been melancholy, and Kazem pulled me out of it, planted in me the warm feeling of homecoming. This kindhearted man, full of good will, who was self educated, had abandoned life in the tribe and went to settle in Baghdad to work in commerce. He was an ardent disciple of Taha Hussein and al-'Aqad, a regular reader of *al-Hilal* and *al-Mouqtataf*, which in those days proved inexhaustible sources to get acquainted with Western culture. "If it weren't for the Christians we wouldn't have become so open to the modern world," he told me. He read Salama Moussa's publications regularly, and had a special admiration for Shibli Shmaile's socialist doctrine, where he found no contradiction with Islamic principles of justice. "In Iraq, the Jews play a similar role in culture and literature," he said, and favorably mentioned Assad Nissim and his magazine, *al-Rassid*. When I told him that Assad was my fellow-townsman and that we were friends, he asked to hear more about him.

What could I tell him of Assad? He had been a dear friend to me, and we shared wonderful childhood experiences in al-Hila. The Great War separated us when his family moved to Baghdad, then I myself traveled to Beirut, and from there to the United States. We kept in touch all those years, and on my return he took me into his house and helped me get by my first days. This was not the same Assad I had known as a child, not the bewildered boy who stayed in the background, but a self-confident man, a successful lawyer, and editor of a literary magazine that drew in all the best writers. Yet he remained, fundamentally, a genuine Hilawi, in his good temper, his sensitivity, and his loyalty. He welcomed me back with a beautiful greeting in his magazine, introduced me to his friends at the Zawaraa club, and invited me there to lecture. He also stood by my side when the family scandal broke out and supported me throughout, even though we no longer shared the same ideas we used to. But as things got more complicated with me, dark clouds rolled into the space of our friendship. I didn't tell Kazem of this, nor did I tell him of the separation from Jane, I only said that she stayed on with her parents to continue medical treatment. This was my response whenever somebody in Baghdad asked about her, until the questions petered out. Some time later when I did tell him the truth and told him that I'd turned my back on a life of convenience in America and a university career, he responded with a smile: "You can no longer surprise me."

I met Kazem in the days before Iraq recovered from the shock of Faisal's death, and naturally we had an exchange of views about the man and his work. Kazem was among the opponents to Faisal's coronation, for in his eyes Faisal was nothing more than a prince in search of a kingship. After he was thrown out of Syria, the British found him a crown in Iraq. "It was an insult," he told me, "and in those days I tended to support keeping Turkish rule despite all its defects, just so we wouldn't be a British colony with a flag, a king, a parliament, and all the other window dressing of a fake national regime. Yet, bit by bit, I learned about this man's virtues, he had a vision and honestly wished to advance Iraq, to unite the people and put an end to tribal conflicts."

I still remember scenes from the rebellion against the Turks in and around al-Hila. I remember the cruel acts of oppression, the public hangings, and the fearful flight to the fields of the governor's mercenaries. The Jews also opposed Faisal's coronation, but for entirely different motives: they wanted direct British rule and were afraid they'd be harmed under Arab Muslim rule but, having failed to dissuade the British from their plan, they collaborated with the King and were among his loyal cronies. Kazem did not appreciate Jewish support of Faisal, but he later came to justify it. "More than they wished to collaborate," he said, "the new regime needed them as the most educated group, able to take on positions in the new administration. Faisal chose well. Sasson Yehezkel was the man who bolstered Iraq's economy. Was there anyone as qualified to be the Minister of the Treasury?"

Talking with Kazem was like a cure for my soul, but when I returned to my room and got into bed I found myself contemplating the visit to New Orleans again, and I couldn't get to sleep. A perverse spirit seizes me whenever the events of that trip stand before my eyes.

Even today, after all the years that have gone by, my heart binds together when I recall that painful affair which changed the course of my life.

AFTER WALKING JANE'S PARENTS to the car and coming back to the apartment, I started gathering the cups and the empty plates, taking as long as I could to wash them in the kitchen because I needed a breather before responding to her father's unexpected proposal. The visit was over and I was leaving for New York in two days, to board the ship for the journey back. My efforts didn't persuade her father—he had plans of his own to guarantee our future, according to his ideas. A rancher and businessman, a typical American, he patronized everyone around him and, from the very beginning of our acquaintance, managed to diffuse my worries. "We love you, you are like a son to us, and you belong with us," he told me over and over. An only daughter and a first grandson, what argument could I pose against their desire? And would it be easy for Jane to disappoint them and go back to a world that rejected her rudely and with malice?

I told her, after she put Jamil to bed in his room: "People don't realize that an invitation to immigrate has to it more insult than care."

She sat, one leg crossed under her, on the big couch, a cigarette between two fingers. "You're offended that my father cares for you?" She looked at me reproachfully.

"He cares for you," I replied immediately, and added with a tone of irony: "and for Jamil, that he doesn't grow up in a backward country."

She tilted forward nervously to tip the ash into the ashtray, not responding. She looked tired and impatient, and I barricaded myself in the chair across from her, the round table separating us. "In fact, I have no complaints," I said after a brief silence, "he is a good father, and I respect him, as you know."

She didn't like to have her parents criticized, and I had no such intention. They acted wisely and accepted me warmly in spite of everything that had happened. I certainly had no complaints about them, on the contrary—I very much appreciated their behavior, and told Jane more than once that, before we got married, in my first lecture at the Zawaraa club, about marital customs in America, it was her parents I was thinking of when I spoke of the liberal approach of parents who don't interfere with their children's choice of a spouse. In fact, I wasn't sure then whether they would disappoint us, but they not only agreed that she marry a foreigner whom they didn't know, they also didn't stand in her way when she decided to travel to me to get married. They tried to convince her, to warn her of the difficulties she would face, but having witnessed her resolve they generously equipped her with everything she needed and even sent the old nanny with her. Maybe they considered it the whim of a spoiled girl who would come back of her own volition once she discovered that I, a year and half after returning to Baghdad, was not quite the man of her dreams. But that's not what happened. Jane went back to them at the end of two years, a baby in her arms.

Ailing and full of disappointment she went back because of an unsuccessful pregnancy, and failed medical treatment, and during the four months with her parents she sent me many letters of longing, entreating me to come. I was already beginning to have my doubts, but I tried to act as if her return was guaranteed. I even decided to remodel the house in Bab al-Sheikh, the house into which I'd moved the first year of my return from America, and which I didn't leave until 1944. It was a six room house, of which only four rooms—three on the top floor and one on the ground floor—were in use, while the remaining two were in a state of disrepair. Together with the attic and the basement they were used to store basic food supplies and things that were seldom used. There was a tall palm tree in the big courtyard that cast scattering shadows. We used to sit there in the hot summer days, hardly ever going up to the rooms. I didn't have a proper study, and I'd made up my mind to clear out the two run-down rooms on the ground floor and make myself a spacious office, somewhat apart from the other rooms. I also made sure to enlarge the living room, and replace the tiles in the bathroom. I wrote Jane about all these changes, not forgetting to mention how envious people would be when she came back. To immigrate? Abandon everything and leave? Cut myself off from my world and seek absorption in an alien society? It angered me to be treated as a stateless person, without a homeland. "Why don't you go to Palestine," Professor Robert Adams of Johns Hopkins University asked me when I paid him a courtesy call. I had studied with him for two years and completed my doctoral dissertation under his supervision, but it took him five years to be surprised at hearing I was Jewish. "They need young talented people like you," he said.

"I suppose your father wouldn't object if we went to Palestine," I took a sarcastic tone and instantly regretted hurting her unintentionally yet again. I was sure she'd told him of this conversation, but personally I saw no point in telling him. As it was I tried avoiding any unnecessary arguments with him. He was a man who saw the world differently than I did; his relationship to me depended on the genuine concerns he had for his daughter, and in his scale of values my national allegiance was outranked by the education I had acquired. "You really are one of us," he often told me, "your English is better than mine, and you don't look at all like an Arab." Had I been a Negro, would he have said such things to me? I'm sure that in spite of his liberal views he would have forbidden his daughter to see me. Prejudice isn't easily uprooted, and I cautiously refrained from answering so as not to find myself in an unpleasant situation. Actually, I held it in his favor that he didn't launch an attack on me, and even welcomed me in spite of the bitter sorrow I caused his daughter. Tell him he's prejudiced? That he offends me in his attempt to compliment me by saying I look American and not like an Arab? Still, it was hard for me to accept, to withdraw and admit my defeat.

"Getting this sort of advice is insulting," I told Jane. "I didn't go to Professor Adams looking for a job or trying to resolve my personal problems."

"But he's your teacher—you always spoke of him with such admiration," she replied.

"Right, I still admire him, but look what happened as soon as he found out I wasn't a Muslim like he thought. All of a sudden I don't belong to a people, a homeland, a culture, I'm just a Jew!"

"You're too sensitive," she sighed.

"I just ask that you understand me. If you were in my place, you would have felt the same humiliation."

Jane gave me a piercing look. Her face was pale and taut, and I realized too late that I'd said what was forbidden for me to say. "I know what you're thinking," I tried to correct myself, "you can also ask me how I'd feel in your place. And you'd be right. Absolutely right."

"I didn't say anything," she turned her gaze to the window, whose pane was slowly being covered by tiny raindrops.

"You didn't say anything, but should I keep quiet? So far I've shut up. I took the poison and kept quiet. I saw you suffer and kept quiet, I was humiliated in public and kept quiet, but not anymore. I have an account to settle with my brother and I'll see it through to the end!"

"Our life is the best answer to your brother," she said in a frail voice, her eyes still fixed on the window.

Indeed, that was true. That's how it was until she left. But once she went back to her parents the chatter began behind my back: the family rejected her, and he couldn't hold on to her. And what would they say when I come back without her? Will the well-wishers try to appease Reuben again? Will they tell him this doesn't look good for a good family? That life in America has distorted my judgment? That I made a mistake and I should admit it? That we should forgive and forget, make peace, because we're brothers? Forgive? Who should forgive whom? Would I be able forgive him? And how would that make me look? I felt trapped—even if I chose to stay in America, Reuben would clap his hands: See! He ran away! A wayward son that has rejected the Jewish people!

Looking at Jane, who went on gazing at the thin raindrops falling on the window pane, I thought that if there was any sense at all in this mess, it was her words that made the most sense. Here we are together, in the apartment her father had bought us, our son sleeping in his bed. As if nothing happened, and we will go on being together, loving each other, raising Jamil, making her parents happy. And what would interrupt us? Of what import is Reuben and his plots against a stable marriage? And a man like me, what more could he wish for than partnership in an architectural firm, American citizenship, and a sure university position? I was thirty two, and all I had achieved was my rank as a civil engineer, with good wages, granted, and senior status, but still a clerk, which I would probably remain. A doctor. The doctor said, the doctor suggested, we should ask the doctor. That's all I have, a title with no substance.

"Jane," I called out in a trembling voice, "will you come with me to Boston tomorrow?"

"I suggested that myself," she said immediately.

"But on the condition that you come back to Baghdad with me!"

She let out a surprised laugh, and I added: "I don't want to go back on my own. It's hard for me to go back to being alone. And I would need your help, don't you think?"

Her laughter suddenly became happy. "You don't know how like you Jimmy is!"

"I'm serious!"

"So am I. Really, he looks like you when he stares like this with those big pleading eyes. He's curious about everything!"

Her cheerful voice pleased me, even though it sounded affected and unnatural. I gave up on pursuing this conversation and said that Jimmy had blue eyes, like hers. Then I said I wouldn't want him to be short-sighted like me, and told her of my distress at school when I was unable to read from the board until I got fitted with glasses, which only worsened my condition. The kids called me *Abu-'Awaynat*, and this nick name stuck to me throughout primary school.

"Jimmy won't be harassed here," she said.

"Here?" I recoiled.

Her gaze slid back toward the window. "I hope it'll be pretty tomorrow," she said, anxiety in her voice.

INVOKING THE MEMORY OF those days, I do not ask, the way some writers of memoirs do, whether I could have acted differently. There is something unfair in this rhetorical question, because it leads to one of two answers: either self-congratulatory praise for good deeds, if there were any, or a search for excuses to cover errors rendered blunt by time. In both cases, the author is winking at the reader, as if to say: See how impossible it was for me to act differently under those circumstances? To lay the blame for mistakes on circumstances, on external factors that cannot be controlled, is not only an evasion of frank confession, but also a fake and despicable form of self-righteousness. For man always finds himself "in circumstances," and his actions can only be the outcome of his disposition toward those circumstances. Man is responsible for his actions, responsible for every mistake he makes in his life, whether in haste or out of consideration, and it is in this responsibility, I think, that he realizes his personal liberty. This liberty, however, is limited, because man can not evaluate his own actions while he is still alive. He can't look at himself from the outside while walking down his one way road, unable to turn left or right. He is in perpetual motion or, more accurately, in a state of being moved by a force which—external as it may seem—is concealed and bound within him. Fate? I call it fate, for this force is simultaneously the source and the outcome of every movement; it is internal energy constantly replenishing itself, like the phoenix that burns and rises from the ashes.

Sometimes I imagine two parallel paths, the one I followed, and the one I might have followed, and like in a jigsaw puzzle I put together an imaginary story that stood no chance of coming true, then take it apart. The two characters walking down the two paths are no different one from the other except in the sphere of illusion, because an inseparable unity connects them, a unity of feeling and purpose. Of course my life might have been different had I chosen to stay in America, but wouldn't I be contemplating it the way I am now, telling myself that I couldn't have foreseen what was to come, and that what did take place was nothing but the outcome of the unceasing movement at work within me?

I asked Jane not to come to New York with me. I told her that farewells at ports wrench my heart, and I wanted to remember only that first farewell of ours, drenched in promise. I also told her I wanted to preserve the memory of our breathtaking meeting in the port of Beirut. Two ports, two pictures with us in them, and Jane in my arms, penetrating my soul, the odor of her hair, soaked in sea wind, setting my passions afire. I told her, I see you drawing farther from me in the port of New York and alighting from the ship with your nanny in the port of Beirut, I want to remember no other image. I told her, let's think of our next meeting in Beirut. All the while I felt like someone else was speaking from within me. I wanted to believe it would be so, that so it must be. And Jane wept, and promised. But on my own in New York, and on boarding the ship, I was trapped in the thicket of my doubts and overtaken by the melancholy air of one who leaves his past behind, his most beautiful years, embarking on a road of no return. A chapter in my life had ended, and even if I found myself in Jane's company once again, I told myself, I would no longer be the same passionate, care-free young man.

I became resentful and spent my time reading, writing letters to Jane and staring at nothing, opaque and paralyzed. I shared my reflections with Jane, trying to find solace in recalling my days at the university, venturing far into my childhood in al-Hila. I told her that if I were a writer I would follow in the steps of Balzac and Hardy, focusing my work on the city of my birth, and on that region known as the middle Euphrates, molding the heroes out of my memories of youth and childhood. But I'm not a writer, and all I have are memories. To tell you the truth, even then I had thought of putting my life story in writing, a story not bereft of its own unique qualities. The story of a Jewish boy from a sleepy town on the bank of the Euphrates, put through the trial of breaking two frames that held him tight, like bands, the tribal separatist frame, and the local traditional frame; from Jewish existence to existence in general, and from the latter to the expanses of human civilization. Many books came out in those days by Arab authors and intellectuals, describing the arduous personal experience of this transition from the Orient westward, opening out from a stagnant civilization toward the universal, and I found the Jewish voice missing among all these Muslim and Christian voices. But were I to write of my own experience, I thought it would be easier to do it in English, for I was still caught in the norms of my early upbringing which prevented me from revealing myself to relatives or friends and acquaintances who might embarrass me with a scolding, as though I were slandering them in the eyes of strangers. I was in a deep fog, and other than the elaborate letters to Jane laden in longing, I didn't write a thing.

I usually wake up before dawn, and throughout this sea journey I would come out on deck to watch the sunrise. Very few people were there at that hour, and being lonely in the emptiness, unlike being lonely in a crowd, set my spirit wondrously soaring. I followed the motion of the waves, rising and breaking into glistening shards, the colors changing in a single wave when a narrow sun beam touched its blue curl. Everything moves and is replaced, all squirms and quivers, the blue aspires to purple and the purple takes on a deep greenness, for just the bat of an eye, immediately turning into sparkling pink and back into the bluish brown that crowns a wave before it collapses into a snow-like sizzle. A motion that repeats itself in countless variations over the infinite expanse, a motion of colors whose order you can never determine, nor the rhythm of their passing. Looking at these sights I would sometimes be grabbed by an almost physical anxiety, as if I were witness to the creation of the world, and the spirit of god moved upon the face of the waters. One morning I was shaken from this gazing to find a Jesuit priest near me, also looking at the sunrise. I told him:

"Whoever can grasp this motion with his senses will be master of his fate."

He regarded me for a long time with a wondrous smile. "Why master fate?" He asked, "is it not better to extricate oneself from fate?"

"To extricate oneself?" I was surprised. "Can man extricate himself from his destiny?"

"Thanks to faith, one can," he replied with satisfaction, his face to the sea. "It purifies emotion and creates harmony between the body and the soul. The faithful man is a free man."

"We are all free men," I insisted, "but who among us can foresee the outcome of his actions?"

"That's not important, it's the ability to overcome the confusion of emotion and bodily temptation. The power to choose is the highest gift the creator gave man, to choose between good and evil."

"But man is not free to judge his own actions, and choosing good does not always yield good. Man is sometimes punished without committing any wrong."

"He is not punished," the priest replied in his monotonous voice, "he is put through the trial of faith, he is purified."

I told him that I would be willing to accept this interpretation, if the clergy didn't aid sinners by instructing them to absolve their misdeeds through charity, prayers, or harmless light fasts. In this way, instead of rooting out sin, they perpetuated it. "But I have something else on my mind," I added. "Look at the motion of these waves. It appears to be repetitive, but in fact it never recurs with any regularity, it is always surprising, leaving you full of anticipation. Such is the state of man, who imagines himself calculating his moves to the last detail, while he is moved by an unfathomable force that inhabits him, and which he can not control. What is this force if not fate? To break away from your fate through faith is nothing but illusion, for you can't break free of destiny except by mastering it. The truly free man, the perfect man, is the one who can say at the end of his days: I am my own fate!"

We kept this conversation going back and forth for a long time. We came to a sort of understanding between ourselves, and from that morning on, for the three or four days we sailed together, I enjoyed our exchanges on deck and in the dining room. He was a pleasant man, a Breton who had already served in Latin America (in Brazil and Peru, it now seems to me), and was on his way to Alexandria as a missionary to the schools there. I told him that while studying in Beirut I discovered Christianity, about which, until then, I had only the vaguest notion. I had known no Christians in my native town, and even in Baghdad I only had a few Christian friends, and our conversations never went beyond general issues. But in Beirut I was in the company of Christians and was invited, for the first time in my life, to the students' Christmas celebration, in which Muslims and Jews also participated. It was also in Beirut that I read the New Testament for the first time, forbidden when I was a child, and this revelation—I told him— widened the horizons before me. Thanks to this revelation, I was drawn to study the history of monotheistic religions during my years of study in America.

This priest, whom I never saw again, nor ever tried to track down, was the only person on the boat I talked with. Now, when I strain to recall those distant days, I grow even more convinced in the power of destiny to determine a man's path. I am also convinced that as a Jew, in those years, and due to the circumstances I was in, I could take no other road than the one I took. I was eager to learn and each new revelation excited me and required me to choose a stance, to examine myself in its light. My upbringing at home restricted me with a wall of terms and customs that I was forced to follow even though I found them hard to put up with. But in the years I had spent at my uncle's house in Baghdad, to continue my education at the *Alliance* school, and even more so after going to Beirut, far away from my family, I grew more curious to understand the world around me, and I was drawn to get to know Christianity and deepen my knowledge of the foundations of Islam. Still, I wasn't free to choose my course of studies after passing the matriculation exam at the American University with flying colors. Medicine was what Jewish families desired, and naturally I had intended to be a physician, but due to delays in the shipping of documents I was prevented from enrolling in medical school when I arrived in New York, and was forced to choose between waiting a whole year, or going to engineering school. I didn't want to inflame my brother's wrath, after he warned me not to throw away a year. So destiny toyed with me, and instead of a physician I became an engineer.

My brother sent me money every month to cover expenses and tuition, and I kept my promise to occasionally send him detailed lecture summaries and report on the progress of my studies. The school of engineering I attended during the first two years was affiliated with the United States Defense Department, and later, when I transferred to a school of civil engineering, I made up my mind to deepen my education in history, and the history of religion. I enrolled in university classes that awarded me, at the end of the semester, a tuition scholarship for an essay on Christian influences in Islam that I had submitted. I was about to complete the requirements for engineering and had to choose between returning to Baghdad or pursuing advanced studies at the renowned Johns Hopkins University. I wrote to my brother asking his consent for an extended stay, but he replied curtly and angrily that I should come back immediately, or else I would never see another penny from him. This was the first sign of the rift between us. The animosity he bore for me also stemmed from the envy he felt for my having acquired higher education while he, the eldest, had taken responsibility for the family upon himself after my father died. Indeed, he was still young when he was taken into my father's business—leasing out the farm lands that belonged to the wealthy Daniel family in al-Hila and its environs. Yet, he always acted like the one who sacrificed himself and gave up his studies for the family and for me, the youngest brother. His response hurt me, because he wasn't sponsoring my stay in America out of his own pocket but out of my part of the inheritance, and I made up my mind from thereon not to ask for his opinion and simply do what I considered best. I must have needed this dispute to guarantee my independence, and it didn't even matter to me if he were to fleece me of my part in the inheritance. In those days I had also won a $250 prize in a writing contest whose subject was pre-military education—part of the curriculum in the engineering school I had attended in the first two years—and this prize encouraged me to stick to my decision and extend my stay by two more years. Reuben stopped sending me money, and I made it my custom to address my letters to my mother and not to him, even though he would read them before reading them aloud to her.

Relations with Reuben deteriorated from that point on but, at least until the shameful scandal he provoked, I kept hoping he would act sensibly, if only out of consideration for my mother. He was a quarrelsome, narrow minded man, consumed by hate. I also hated him, and after the separation from Jane I became vengeful, but the more I turned over ways to hurt him as he had hurt me in my mind, the more I was deterred from doing anything that might add to my mother's suffering, beyond the suffering she had already borne in silence. I was unhappy on the ship, unhappy and depressed, and I recall that in moments of conversation with the Jesuit priest I felt more than once the urge to unveil the affair with my brother, but my shyness stopped me, and he showed no tendency to discuss personal matters, preferring to converse on abstract philosophical issues. He was an educated man, and his deep familiarity with Judaism and Islam surprised me, along with his wide knowledge of the culture of Greece and Neo-Platonism. On the last day before he stepped off the ship in the port of Alexandria, we talked at length of ancient Egyptian civilization, and how unfamiliar it was to Islam, not being affected as much by it as it was by Greek civilization. I told him this was a loss for Islam, but that Europe, which owes a great debt to Muslim civilization, tried to repudiate Islam for generations, and represented Muslims as barbarians. I must have spoken enthusiastically, for his response was something between mock surprise and someone hesitating to assert a fact: "You talk like a Muslim!" I told him: "Must I be a Muslim to acknowledge the facts?" And he immediately corrected himself and asked my forgiveness for the offense. "You didn't offend me," I replied, "I even see this as a compliment, even though I was born a Jew, I see the best in each religion and do not adhere to any of them."

Some encounters should remain without a sequel. Such was the encounter with that priest. Two years later, when I spent nearly three months in Egypt, I saw no point in trying to contact him.

I AWOKE AT THREE-TWENTY from a twisted and tortuous dream. I was in a dimly lit hall, and many people came in through its entryway, having to go through narrow ruined alleys, and here I was myself trying to make my way through these alleys and getting nowhere. The bedside lamp was on and the book I had been reading lay on my chest. I had fallen asleep while reading, as sometimes happens, but when I switched off the light and turned to the wall, I suddenly remembered the new video player that broke down, and Butheina couldn't find the warranty. A silly incident, and I don't know how she managed to infect me with her worries over it, that without the warranty the company wouldn't respect its commitment to fix the machine, even though the date of purchase could easily be tracked. So I began speculating that the warranty might have still been in my hands, but even after dismissing these speculations I was left in a sort of anticipation that chased the sleep away from my eyes.

I turned the light back on, and took the book. Reading only made me more alert, and an hour later I felt the need to go to the toilet. I put on my robe and walked carefully, leaving the door slightly ajar to let just enough light out to make my way through the dark corridor. Hamida was snoring in her regular high pitched staccato but when I passed by her room she called me. "Go on sleeping," I told her. And she replied: "I'm not asleep," and coughed.

I'm puzzled by Hamida's sleep. She falls asleep quickly and snores incessantly, but upon my every move she wakes up and claims she isn't sleeping. How I envied her, and how it annoyed me in the first months of our marriage.

When I came back from the toilet she called me again. "You aren't asleep either?"

"I woke up," I said and walked on to my room.

"I'm thinking of the girl. She'll be left without a father again."

I didn't reply. Sabry isn't going yet and she's already haunted by worries. When he does go away, the old refrain will resume: She doesn't eat, see how pale she is, all children have a father and she doesn't! I told Butheina, You can rely on me not to stand in your way. But she knows her mother won't let her move out. Ever since they moved in with us, her life is centered round the grandchild. Parting with them wouldn't be easy for me either, but it makes Butheina miserable. Mother spoils my girl with her behavior, instills in her a dependence on her father, and I'm just powerless! True. But I can't be of help.

I sit by the desk. Four hours of sleep is enough. The rain beats strongly on the neighboring garage's tin rooftop. The roar of a bus rises from afar. Early rising workers head for the morning shift. At this very hour, I also used to get out to construction sites when I worked for the city. The guard would take me into his shack and serve me a glass of refreshing tea. I loved being on site before daylight. The maps spread out in front of me, the blue prints hanging on the wall. I was like a general in his headquarters, commanding the situation, filled with a sense of self esteem. All that is gone. But the habit of rising before dawn never left me, it was just supplemented by troubled sleep helped along with pills. The memories remain, and that is what I do now, recount my memories as they come up in my mind, bit by bit, without order.

And here's what sprang to the surface of my memory:

The voice was annoyed, beseeching and hostile: "Why do you drive us away? Where are we to go?"

I was in the company of the district officer and two contractors when the man caught me coming out of the cafe. I told him there's a plan, and we work by the plan, but he grabbed my jacket and yelled in a Jewish accent: "Over our houses of all places? Can't you move the road a little?"

He was agitated, and must have been laying in wait for me to pour his heart out. The district officer and the contractors regarded the man with an amused smile, and my assistant rushed to my side: "What's the matter? What does he want?" I felt distressed. We were in the very heart of al-A'admiyah, where many knew of my Jewishness. "I do not determine the course of the road," I calmly told him.

"You're the Chief Engineer, you're in charge, tell them!" He pointed at the district officer with his hand.

"You will be compensated," the assistant told him.

"Who'll be compensated?" The man replied angrily. "The land-lords will, but us, where should we go? All Jews are like me, you want to drive us out!"

I began to worry that should he continue in this vein things might come to a bad end. The situation was already tense enough. The papers published articles demanding that Jews be expelled from this holy neighborhood, and constructing the road was taken to be in compliance with this demand, even though the project had been ready and waiting in city offices for a few years. Road building through ancient quarters always caused riots, the landlords incited the tenants, and the tenants attacked the workers and city inspectors. I felt no joy taking on the responsibility for work in this neighborhood, I was afraid of being harassed because of being Jewish, but the landlords showed no resistance because the houses slated for demolition were mostly populated by Jews who thought twice before rioting.

Passersby stopped next to us, and some people came out of the cafe to see how things would end up. "Go home," I told him, try-ing to free my jacket from his grip.

"Go to the Jewish quarter," one of the crowd called out to him.

"There'll be only Muslims here, you hear?" Another pushed him off me and nearly knocked him to the ground.

"Come, let's go," the assistant pulled me by the arm.

I lingered a little, because the man looked scared, and I was scared of the crowd unleashing its anger on him, but we hadn't gone more than a few steps before he caught up with us and grabbed my jacket again: "You behave like them. You sit with them in their cafes and drink from their cups, you are not one of us!" His voice trembled and his eyes burned with bottomless hatred.

All I wanted was for him to spit in my face, and not due to the demolition of his home or the expulsion of the Jews from the neighborhood, only because I was different. Many Jews were like that man, and were annoyed by the respect with which I was treated in the company of Muslims. The cafe where I was sitting bore a sign up front, "For Muslims Only," and this in itself was enough to see me as not one of them, to even see me as condescending and conspiring with their oppressors against them. At first, working for the city, I tried to reduce my involvement in Muslim society and conceal it, but over time I learned that the more I tried to be considerate of the Jews' sense of frustration, the more they increased their animosity toward me.

"A madman, don't pay attention," the assistant said.

"Yes, a madman," I replied unwillingly.

AT SIX I WENT downstairs to wash. Hamida was already standing in the kitchen and served me carrot juice. "You don't look well," she said in her worried tone.

"The rain disturbed my sleep," I replied.

"The mind disturbed you, not the rain," she looked at me reproachfully.

I asked her if the warranty was not, by any chance, in the closet in her room, and she replied angrily: "Since when do I keep warranties? Is this what worries you?"

"I know what worries you," I replied.

"So give me an answer. Can you?"

"No one has an answer. Do you think we haven't talked about it enough?"

"You're avoiding the issue, only wrapped up in your own things, it's as if you don't care about the girl."

I didn't reply. I'm already used to such rebukes. But this time she caught me off guard with her demand: "You have to write to Jamil," she said, and lit a cigarette.

For a week she's been grunting about America. She said nothing to Sabry, but in his absence she never stops voicing her astonishment at Jamil's invitation to host him in New York. Butheina doesn't reply, and I try to assuage her by saying that for Jamil, Sabry is still part of the family. "What do you want me to write to him?" I asked.

"Explain it to him. He'll understand. He too is a father of children."

"Write him to cancel the invitation?"

She took a long puff on her cigarette, and replied without looking at me: "Jamil knows about growing up without a father."

"I'm guilty, I'm always guilty," I said, wanting to conclude the conversation.

"Guilty or not, the girl needs a father. Why America of all places? What does he miss here? He's been offered a job in the Ministry of Agriculture, a respectable job. You have to talk to him. You can influence him."

"And have you thought about Butheina?"

"You're asking me if I've thought about Butheina?"

"She's still young, we have to think of her future."

"But she has a girl!"

"Alright, talk to her," I replied and turned to go.

"She doesn't have to know. Write to Jamil in my name, if it makes you feel bad. If I could write to him myself I wouldn't have asked you."

She managed to upset me first thing in the morning. What doesn't she think of in order to hold onto Sabry. If I write to Jamil, all I can do is plead with him to urge Sabry to travel sooner. For two months he's been roaming around doing nothing, talking about going into business or resuming his studies, and in the mean time he spends every day with us. This can't go on much longer. I like him a lot, and I enjoy his company, but his visits create a problem, even his father has insinuated that he's getting uncomfortable. Jamil's invitation came at the right time, and if I do have any influence over him—I thought—I'm obliged to urge him to go, to stay away from home.

Chance had it—and our lives are nothing but a chain of incidents—that a few hours later I was to witness the risk of him staying any longer.

At nine I had to go out for a board meeting at the Academy of the Arabic Language, but before going out I called the Hasoon Brothers Company, who promised to send a technician to check the video player, and should it be found faulty, replace it. They didn't even ask about the warranty, and Butheina's apprehensiveness was, as usual, unnecessary. Every little problem acquired disastrous proportions, and somehow she managed to pass her apprehensiveness on to those around her, especially me.

The day turned out to be full of surprises and anxiety for me. The board meeting that was supposed to discuss terminology in the new botanical dictionary dealt with an entirely different subject:

marking the fortieth anniversary of the Academy's foundation! Even before entering the building I was surprised to find policemen and security guards blocking the entry to the square in front, and when I inquired what this meant I was told that the Minister of Culture was about to arrive. It turned out that only half an hour earlier the Minister had announced his desire to attend the meeting, news that scared Moustafa al-Sharbati, who called up the accountant, assuming the Minister wanted to discuss the budget. The financial report wasn't ready yet, and according to our understanding with the Ministry chiefs we were to present it at the beginning of the next month. We gathered in al-Sharbati's office, and together with the accountant prepared an estimated balance that would please the Minister, but to our surprise the Minister had no intention of discussing the budget. Into the silence that descended on us he dropped his proposal to mark the Academy's forty years with celebratory events that none of us could have thought up in our wildest imagination. There's no guessing as to who whispered this idea in the Minister's ear, and whether he really intended to celebrate the event with much pomp, with poetry and music festivals, with spectacular light and sound shows in the ruins of Babylon in the presence of the President and guests from abroad!

We listened to him, astounded. Since when does an Academy of the Arabic Language, which ought properly to celebrate its own establishment at academic conferences or by publishing a special issue of its periodical and other academic publications, have need for such festivities that have nothing to do with its own work? But, as usually happens in meetings with Ministers and other men of power, words of praise and flattery didn't take long to start breaking the silence with which the Minister's words were received. Moustafa al-Sharbati, the first to set the tone, tried, in his function as secretary, to be practical, and proposed the election of a committee, comprised of members of the Academy and a representative of the Ministry of Culture that would work out a detailed plan for the celebrations. The Minister listened, somewhat smugly, to what the participants had to say, and then, looking at me and smiling, said: "I have a candidate for chairing the committee, the eldest member, and one of the original founders of the Academy!" This wasn't something I expected. I of all people, I who remained silent only to show my lack of enthusiasm at the idea—I was embarrassed, especially as it was clear to me that Moustafa was eager to preside over this national celebration. But the Minister's words were taken for a decision that all supported, including Moustafa, who told me: "The Minister said what we were all thinking."

The Minister left us right after this, and the members went on talking of the festivities, and, of course, we never got to discuss botanical terminology. At the end of the meeting Jawad al-'Alawi told me jokingly: "From now on Moustafa will be more careful about making suggestions in the Minister's presence." I told him I felt awkward not to have apologized to him, and he laughed: "To apologize for the Minister? Give him a free hand, that would be his compensation!" Indeed, that's what I would do. As secretary of the Academy, he would be in charge of the celebrations.

All this now strikes me as farcical next to the fear that descended upon me a few minutes later. It was near noon, and on leaving the building I found Sabry waiting for me by the gate. "I thought you'd have a hard time finding a taxi in the rain," he greeted me with his friendly smile.

The first thought that came to my mind was that Hamida had told him something about going away, for he didn't usually pick me up after meetings. It hadn't even rained since morning and the taxi stand was only about a hundred meters from the building. "Have you been to the house?" I asked.

"And how would I know you were here?"

"What brings you here?" I held his arm.

"The car is around the corner," he said, ignoring the question, "They didn't let anyone get near the place until the Minister's car left."

We walked to the car silently and it was only after he fired the engine and we began moving that he revealed the reason for his visit. Zuhair had been arrested, and apparently many arrests were made last night. "They say it's drug related," he added, "But I don't believe it."

"And how did you find out?" I asked.

"I called him this morning, and his mother asked me to come over. Don't ask what a state I found her in. She doesn't know why he was taken and who was arrested with him."

Dumbfounded and confused, I told him: "You too must be under surveillance now."

Sabry gave me a stunned look and didn't reply. My comment was out of place and I felt sorry for making it. Zuhair was his close friend, a member of the Maoist circles and an activist in the student union. He met him through Butheina. As a child he was like family. Qassem's adopted son, he's like a brother to Butheina! How would she take this terrible news?

"We have to do something," Sabry said, "at least to find out what he's accused of."

"Could it be drugs?"

"What do you mean drugs? They're breaking his bones as we speak!"

I kept quiet. It was clear to me that Badriya asked him to let me know, and wasn't it natural that she ask me for help?

I WAITED UNTIL MIDNIGHT last night for a call from the Minister of the Interior. I rang his office after parting with Sabry and, since I couldn't find him there, I called him at home and his wife promised he'd call me back when he got there. He wasn't aware of the arrests. I told him it had to do with drugs and that was his department. He promised to check and let me know. He just called again. Zuhair is being interrogated by the *Mukhabarat*—that's all he could find out.

ZUHAIR'S ARREST HAS BEEN keeping us busy for days. I approached anyone who might be of help, and it was only today that I heard from Maulud al-Takriti, one of the Ba'athist leaders, who said it's about a group that was in touch with the underground Islamic D'awa party, planning an uprising in the north. I took Sabry with me and drove to see Badriya. The three daughters were there with their husbands, and they all looked at us with unnerving anticipation. I began with empty, calming words, straining to sweeten the bitter pill, and when I finally mentioned what the group was suspected of Badriya let out a horrendous scream: "They're going to kill him! They're going to kill my son!" And she began pulling her hair and running amok around the house. The daughters rushed to her side and held her, but she fought them and kept screaming: "I'll kill myself before they kill my son!" The husbands also tried to subdue her, only Sabry and I remained frozen where we stood, helpless and ashamed.

An only son after three daughters, the husband had died in a road accident when he was merely two months old. Qassem became like a father to him and from early childhood planted the revolutionary seed in him. A communist, a Maoist, and now activity in a group that has contacts with a Shi'ite organization? Sabry keeps denying that Zuhair had any contact with the Iranian exiles, yet he was ready to admit that two years ago, after a visit to Lebanon, Zuhair came back excited by the ideas and personality of Moussa al-Sadr, the charismatic Shi'ite leader who disappeared in Libya. This was two years ago, yet he never tried to contact Khomeini's disciples, all sitting right in Najaf? And what makes Sabry so sure of all this when he was in London most of this time? There's no smoke without fire, though it certainly is hard to grasp such a turn, not to mention how he managed to hide it from the people closest to him! Neither Sabry nor Butheina had noticed any shift in his views, not to mention his mother and the rest of the family. Now additional arrests are being reported. Will interrogation reveal the truth? But whose truth? In today's tense and hazy state all I can do is worry.

How will Qassem react when he hears the news? It would be a fatal blow to him, to have his favorite turn into a supporter of the Islamic revolution! How would he feel, this political exile, the atheist who declared total war against religion? Would he be angry? At whom? At tender-spirited Zuhair, who lost his way? At himself for failing to inoculate him against foreign influence? At the circumstances that separated them and forced him into a life of exile? I remember his words, when the party sent him to the southern marshes and he didn't fast during the month of Ramadan: "I won't pretend," he told me, "They know that a communist believes in the revolution and not a phantom god. I come to them as a teacher, to organize the struggle, and I have no need for them to be like me. This way things are clear, there is no lie, there is trust!"

Qassem 'Abd al-Baqi, my dear friend, the third side of our triangle of friendship in al-Hila. He had become a lawyer by the time

I came back from America. He and Assad Nissim had studied law, but while Assad turned to literature, he began reading Marx. Qassem may have been the only Marxist to support the Bakr Sidqi uprising in 1936, but he quickly changed his mind and began accusing the organizers of the uprising with treason and taking on Nazi sympathies in their policies. I don't know exactly when this shift in his views took place, I was in Cairo at the time, but I have no doubt that Kamel al-Chadarchi's resignation from Hikmat Suleiman's government contributed to his view of the uprising. While he was still a student of law he was among the Ahali group, from which the Democratic-National Party evolved, and he supported al-Chadarchi, the way we all did, as an outstanding leader and a real patriot. And yet he was ill at ease within the group, many of whom were of wealthy landed families, he liked to call them "the Aristocracy." As the son of a poor peasant, he had paved his own path in life; he knew how to plant a hedge between himself and those of good stock who never had a taste of poverty. How could I not remember when, even in those distant days of our childhood, he pronounced our differences. His words, spoken to me at the great celebration of the Hindiya dam, are engraved in my memory. I was swept by the waves of the peasants' joy and, with the excitement of an innocent child, said that I wanted to be a peasant and work the land. And he, not without a little animosity: "You, whose father controls half the city's land, neither you nor Assad would be peasants, nor me either. I'm going to study!"

We were children, and boundless dreams resonated through our world. Assad's family moved to Baghdad during the first year of the Great War, while I was sent, two years later, to my uncle's home in Baghdad, to study at the *Alliance* school. Qassem remained among his people, and we lost touch with each other after I went to Beirut, and from there to the United States. When I came back he was living in a small house in Hayderkhana, together with a loyal servant that stayed with him since he had left al-Hila to come and study in the capital. We were three friends, and each had gone his own way. Assad was at the height of his success as a poet and editor of *al-Rassid*, and Qassem was dedicated to his calling as an attorney, "defender of the wretched," by his own definition. He had paid his own way through school and found communism and underground activism by himself, things that led him to arrests and the atrocious torture in the dungeons of the CID, the British police's Criminal Investigation Department. The 14th of July revolution opened the prison gates for him, and his star shone forth as one of the staunchest defenders of the new regime, but only for a brief moment, until he was hounded again, his flesh flogged by interrogators, until the big escape from the central prison in al-Hila and his departure for exile.

Qassem had been a loner all his life, and he is alone now, in exile, in the evening of his days. I don't know if there's any truth to the story of his love for Badriya. She was only a girl when she moved to Baghdad and landed in his brother Jum'ah's lap, and Jum'ah had three daughters and a son before he died in a road accident. Qassem became the head of the family but remained a bachelor, never marrying Badriya. Zuhair was his favorite son, and he learned about prisons from the time he was an infant, accompanying his mother on visits to the revolutionary uncle. Now he himself is getting a taste of interrogation!

I SHOWED SABRY THE letter I once got from Jamil, following the party at the presidential palace. "I'm proud of you," he wrote, "and I am deeply sorry that mother is no longer among the living."

"He really admires you," Sabry said, "and when I talked to him on the phone from London he sounded moved to learn that you're being paid such respect."

"If he admires me, it's only because his mother brought him up this way, not because I'm worthy of admiration."

"What makes you say such things?" Sabry wondered.

"A son cannot admire a father he grew up without," I replied, spurred on by some urge toward self deprecation.

Sabry's face grew dark as he looked at me, muted. I immediately regretted having said this after advising him to leave for America earlier than planned, considering the situation. "Jamil did make his mother happy, and his grandfather," I quickly added.

"And you as well," he said.

"True, and me as well," I confirmed, without remarking that I had no claim to this happiness.

Why hide behind my words? Have I done anything for him? Did I contribute anything to his upbringing? I ran away. I deserted him at the age of four and became immersed in my own business, in my own wars. I could claim it wasn't just my fault, I could cling to circumstances and win the support of innocents, just as I did when I told Kazem that I had preferred the homeland over family life and a career in America. All this won't change the fact that Jamil grew up without a father.

I didn't sleep that night, and when the alarm clock rang I turned toward the wall and drew the blanket over my head. Jane went to the bathroom, then came back in a minute or two to wake me up. "I'm not going," I told her, and she stayed by the bed, as though reconsidering. I wanted her to say something, to ask why, to reprimand me, but she was silent, and once she left the room I was aware of her every movement. She didn't call her father, as I expected her to, but kept busy in the kitchen for a long time. Then Jamil woke up, and I heard her talking to him, her laughter mixing with his fresh giggle.

At eight the nanny arrived, but I stayed in bed a full hour, my whole body in pain from laying down without sleep. At last I threw off the blanket and got up. "I'm going to New York tomorrow," I told her, and once again she didn't respond. Her silence irritated me. The night before she was determined to accompany me to the architectural firm in Boston, that's why she asked the nanny to come earlier than usual, and now she put on an air of indifference, as though she had anticipated this. Had she come to terms with the separation?—I asked myself. Had she assumed from the beginning that there was no other way out, and only wanted to put me to the test? I was boiling with anger, I felt cheated. I hadn't noticed the change in her, I kept telling myself. I had sought to see my most cherished image of her, but being close to her parents had changed her beyond recognition. They pampered her with love, bought her an apartment nearby so they could see her daily and keep her close to them, so they could act as Jamil's good grandparents. An idea took hold of me at the time, that it was all planned to present me with a done deed, to force me to surrender to their will, to bring me under their protection. Your home is here, your one and only family, and we've invested our money in the architectural firm to make you a stock-holding partner in a prospering business.

I entered the bath and locked the door behind me. It was an awkward time for an argument with Jane, though I don't know that I'd have been up for it if we were alone in the house. To bluntly tell her what raged in my heart? Blame her? Tell her it wasn't during these four months with her parents that she resolved to stay, but long before that? Tell her that even in Baghdad she was preparing not to come back? The questions roared in my mind as I lathered my face in front of the mirror. I was never so angry with Jane as on that morning. I despised myself, a ridiculed innocent husband, deluded enough to put his money and energy into remodeling the house to please his wife, who then dismissed him. Frankly, more than being angry at Jane, I apprehended my situation on returning without her. Any excuse I'd make up would arouse curiosity, and worst of all, Reuben would gloat over my demise. She ditched him, she took his son and kicked him out! That's how everyone would interpret my return. Will they believe me when I say she needs to be under a doctor's care? Is her condition so severe? Is she pregnant, they'll ask, and the doctors advise her to remain under supervision? Any other explanation would arouse questions and curiosity, and yet I couldn't think anything else up.

I am trying to recall every thought that passed through my mind, and a surge of sorrow drowns me. The years have blurred the memories, and only the figure of Jane, in her tender sadness, stands before me, admonishing me. Each hostile thought of her seems nonsensical and unreal, for what I remember is that moment of grace—I was still sliding the razor over my cheek, when the question flittered through my mind: And Jane, would it be easy for her without me? Would it be easy for her to explain the separation? And to go back into the embrace of her parents, was that something to rejoice? Yes, even within the storm of emotion, I couldn't help but think of Jane, and that caused me to speculate and calculate until I found solace in saying that time must be allowed to do its work, and there was no reason to forsake hope. The parents will finally give in and stop pressuring her, when they realize how determined and unwilling to give in to their wishes I was—as long as I retained my dignity, they would understand me and reach a compromise.

These thoughts pacified me and gave me a sense of reconciliation; moreover, they allowed me to feel good about myself. I was already calm, and having finished the shave, made up my mind to salve my aching body with a hot bath. It was only in America that I'd taken to the pleasures of a bath, and even though I didn't usually spend much time soaking since I rushed to wash up quickly, in times of fatigue and depression I found it a trustworthy refuge that built my confidence. I remember thinking of Jane the moment I stepped in the water, and how she found it hard to get used to the absence of a bath tub in the bath room. Indeed, she never complained, and even loved the spacious bath room with the coal-heated floor, but in those days it was unusual to install a bath tub, and I hadn't thought of it when I remodeled the house. It'll be the first thing I do when I get back to Baghdad, I thought, congratulating myself, and immediately decided to announce this to Jane when I got out.

I was already calm enough to harbor such thoughts. My rage was gone, how could one be angry at Jane? I can only think good thoughts of her, only appreciation, and love, and infinite longing fills my heart. Jane withstood the storm, and didn't break down; she suffered the insults, the excommunication and disgrace, and remained by my side, inspiring me with her magnanimity. A Christian woman? You brought us a Christian woman? To stain the family reputation? Are there no Jewish women in America? Reuben screamed, and my mother wailed as though facing a catastrophe. He excommunicated me, and went to the synagogue to demand that I be banished from the community. He even found it in his heart to sit *Shiv'ah* for me, the seven days of mourning for the dead, but my mother did not respond to this and my sister Na'ima supported her. I was a wayward son in their eyes; marrying a Christian woman came close to apostasy and required banishment and public denunciation. My mother bore her grief in silence, and it was only after the scandal had died down that Na'ima found a way to get in touch with me. "Mother loves you," she'd tell me, "She wants to see you and your wife. But how? Reuben forbids her to even mention your name!"

I was torn between love for my mother and love for my wife. I was prevented from seeing my mother, while I would mumble sweet nothings in Jane's ear that I myself was more in need of than she. I told her the Jews are no different from anyone else, and prejudice runs rampant among them. I told her that due to suffering and persecution they shut themselves off and erected a wall of prohibitions to preserve their uniqueness. I added that the religious zeal that had withstood generations, rooted them in the faith that god had chosen *them* from among the nations. Groundless notions, I told her, ideas I did not believe and was even averse to. But she had no need for these questions, she understood, she even forgave, and told me more than once: "I'm sorry you suffer because of me." She was only unable to restrain herself once, when she was prevented from working as an English teacher, and she called out in anger: "That's too much!" But nothing was too much for a grudge-bearing avenger like Reuben. He pulled strings in the Jewish community to make sure her application to teach in one of the Jewish schools was rejected. I couldn't bear to see her distress, and went to see Assad Nissim who stood by me in support. I spoke harshly to him and, as was his wont, he replied politely and tried to calm me down, even suggesting I join him to see the officials in charge of education in the community institutions, but I refused. If they complied with Reuben's intrigues and joined the ban he had imposed on me, they were too low for me to address!

That's what Reuben was like, and that's what the elected Jewish officials and eminent leaders were like—contemptible people, whose faith is based on xenophobia. But all this could have been overcome, and nothing would have clouded our lives if it weren't for the aborted pregnancy and the failure of the doctors. Jane wouldn't have gone back to her parents, and I wouldn't have posed her with that terrible dilemma. I encouraged her to go, even pleaded with her. To me, this trip served to quiet my conscience. I couldn't imagine her father had other plans. It would have been easier for me to find him hostile, had he insulted and chastised me, had he behaved the way a man like him ought to, but he took me in with genuine affection and did all he could to guarantee our future. It was hard for me, banished from my family, to reject the extended hand, the embracing arms of an adoptive family.

Honor. The Eastern man's imaginary honor. The concentric structure of this dilemma, each circle growing out of another, and I among them, circling around myself. I couldn't disregard prevailing notions or refrain from adapting my behavior to accepted norms, even though I was proud of my difference, of being a free man of western customs. Which is precisely how I was seen in that environment, an environment whose relationship to me depended on its willingness to accept me. At the office I was the most highly educated, as well as a Jew and married to an American. Everything about me distinguished me from everyone else, bore a unique mark and set me apart. In those days I was the only engineer educated in the west, the first to hold a doctoral degree from Johns Hopkins University. This is how Assad Nissim introduced me in his paper upon my return: "Dr. Haroun Saussan, the first Iraqi to achieve fame in America," but at the reception he held for me, at the Zawaraa club, he took the liberty to add that I was also the first Jew to do this. In his name, and in the name of the other members, he expressed the community's pride for having one of its sons accomplish all that. This Jewish pride was bestowed on me without my asking for it, along with all the obligation that entailed. And just as it was given, it was withdrawn and brutally trampled upon when the scandal broke out. Indeed, Assad's relations with me didn't change one bit; he even tried to restrain Reuben and protect me, but the scandal reverberated throughout the Baghdad community and I was no longer a source of pride but someone people felt uncomfortable around, someone to stay away from. These were the morals of a tribe, of a closed cult, suspicious of anyone unusual, where the individual wasn't free to diverge from convention. But tribal morals never, and still do not, belong exclusively to Jews. What hurt me even more was disapproval from my Muslim friends both at and away from work. Though they didn't approve of my brother's behavior, and even condemned him in lukewarm terms, it was clear to me that they were willing to see reasons behind it, not due to my marrying a Christian, but due to my marrying an American! The foreigner is never favored, always suspicious. I had to keep my mouth shut and ignore the evasive looks. As the circle of curiosity closed in on me, I had to act as naturally as I could, but on coming home and seeing Jane in her distress and solitude, I'd overflow with guilt and sink into melancholy.

It was hard for a western woman to acclimatize to the way of life in Baghdad. A woman's place was at home, and on going out she was compelled to shroud herself in a black robe and throw a veil over her face. Except for the lower classes, a woman didn't leave the house unaccompanied by her husband, a close family member, or a servant who walked behind her like a body guard. Jane couldn't adapt to this humiliation and preferred to stay shut in at home, where she had no one to talk to but the Kurdish maid. When I would take her with me in the car to visit friends, or for some official function, she couldn't feel at ease because she hardly knew Arabic. But what bothered her in particular were the times she found herself the only woman among men. Their sycophantic behavior disgusted her. They are full of lechery — she'd tell me — they lock up their women and try to win your affection by foolish talk and hidden intentions. The men made her sick, and I had nothing to say in their defense.

"What's the great loss?" She told me. "Four years working for the city, another project, another road construction. An engineer. That's as far as you've gotten. The Ministry of Foreign Affairs is out of reach because you're Jewish. Why won't you admit it? What did you go to school for?"

She was repeating her father's words, and I trust he was even harsher when he spoke to her. With me he was wary of such talk, and on that day he didn't even show a sign of anger or disappointment at my decision not to go to the architectural firm in Boston. "I won't stand in your way, and never intended to," he told me smoothly, "At your age I didn't like advice either, and perhaps, in your place, I wouldn't have been quick to take up the offer I made you either, which doesn't mean I'd be doing the right thing."

A sharp business man, he spoke to the point and gave you a feeling of trust. He added: "Go back to Baghdad, carry on with your duties as a responsible man and a dedicated worker, only remember that my proposal still stands, your place in the Boston group is waiting for you, it was a condition for the contract."

Jane sat tense during this short conversation, but when her father suggested calling a baby-sitter so we could go out with them to a restaurant, her face lit up, and she said she'd ask the nanny to look after Jamil.

"We'll say good bye with dinner," he patted my shoulder as he got up, "more like saying see you soon," he emphasized with a smile.

My mind was scattered because he defied my expectations, and it was only after he left that I told Jane: "I didn't know he already invested in the group," as if that was the only surprise for me in his visit.

Jane didn't reply, but the look on her face made it clear to me that she hadn't known either. But she wasn't surprised. She was used to her father's unflagging energy; she trusted him, and relied on him to emerge the winner out of any situation. It was good for her to find shelter under her father's warm wings, an errant dove returning to the nest after rebelling against him. But I, on the other hand, I'm being asked to join her, or be on my way, alone and dejected. "I haven't heard you call him," I said, trying to shake away these thoughts.

"He rang," she replied.

"I didn't hear his ring either."

"You were taking a bath."

I let out a laugh, and she laughed too, and for a moment we eyed each other in confusion. "I've made up my mind," I said, "to install a bath tub in the bathroom, so there's nothing you won't have when you come."

"That's not what I want," she replied.

"Will you come?"

"We'll see," she lowered her eyes.

I choked. I craved to hold her in my arms, to forget everything and make a fresh start. But I remained frozen where I was, until finally I turned to the bedroom to get dressed. I feel sorry for her, I thought. The month went by quickly, and the future was vague. I should have told her father, See you in Baghdad, but he managed to confuse me and I couldn't respond. He usurped any initiative I might have had with his paternal behavior, always the boss, in charge of things. A friendly farewell, and Jane could be proud of her cunning father. A good girl. Her rebellion didn't cause a rift. She asked them to consider her feelings, and they complied. Sent her off with the nanny and waited. They didn't bother to come themselves, as though they assumed this was nothing but the whim of a dreamy girl. A long range tactic. They sat and waited, children are bound to come back within their own borders. "Jane," I hurriedly called out, rushing to her, "I want you to know I won't give you up!"

"Give me up?" She stammered in astonishment.

"Neither you, nor Jimmy."

"You considered giving us up?"

"I want you to have no such thoughts!"

She pulled me by the arm. "Harry, what's happening to you?"

I drew her to me and hid my face in her soft hair. "I love you, and I can't bear not having you with me."

"I am with you," she said, her body shivering against mine.

"I'll wait for you. Promise?"

"Yes, promise."

"Remember what you told me in Beirut? You said now we're twice married. And the Consul heard you and said I am your witness. Twice married will never separate."

"We won't separate, Harry," came out in a voice fainter than faint.

I held her face in both my hands. "I need you by me, I need your support. I can't stay mute any longer. I won't rest before I settle the account with my brother."

"What does it matter?"

"It matters to me. It has to do with me, it's my world whether I like it or not and I can't just shake it off or it will haunt me the rest of my life!"

Jane put her head against my chest again and I tightened my grip, as though trying to take her inside me and carry her with me wherever I went, through all my struggles, through all the vengeance that made my blood boil.

THE EDITOR OF THE literary show on the radio presented me with a precious gift: a cassette containing Assad Nissim's talks, just as they were aired by the Israeli broadcasting company. "We selected a few segments," he told me, "and got the Minister's approval after he listened to them, but a decision finally came down to postpone the broadcast." I can't figure out what fault they could have found with what he said, when he recounted his childhood in al-Hila, and his extensive literary work. Does anything refute Zionist propaganda about Jews yearning for the land of their fathers more than this strong connection to the homeland, expressed by someone who had been one of its most loyal sons? I listen to his soft voice, saturated with longing, and tears well up in my eyes: here, at this point, we connect again, over a breach of many years, in our love for our native town, the Princess of the Euphrates, as he had eulogized in one of his poems!

Only someone who grew up in al-Hila could speak of his childhood with such feeling, and Assad is a genuine Hilawi, even now in the land of his migration, before enemy microphones that so often broadcast lies, he sticks to his first love, the place that cradled him at birth. That's what Assad is like, and anyone who bears him a grudge for having left should take a lesson from him about loyalty. I will speak more of Assad and his work, but now I am possessed by those childhood experiences, I see the city celebrating the renewed flow of water in the dried up creek. I was twelve, and from early that morning rumor had traveled throughout the Jewish neighborhood that after ten years of hardship the longed for day had arrived, ever since the old dam at al-Hindiya collapsed. My father, a City Council member, attended an urgent meeting at the Turkish governor's office, and I went out after him to see the masses gathered in the central square, deeply moved and incredulous. When the Council members stepped out of the building to announce that work on the new dam had indeed been completed, a great shout of joy erupted, and the women began singing out a long series of praises. "We'll go and see for ourselves," a call rose from the crowd, and soon the gathering dispersed as many made their way to the new dam, some on foot, some on the back of a donkey or a horse. I rushed to my father who stood among the dignitaries and asked his permission to ride his noble mare to witness the opening of the dam. He smiled and lingered before answering but I knew he'd find it hard to refuse me under the circumstances, just as he would surely have said no if he was alone.

I galloped toward al-Hindiya and was among the first to gather on a hill overlooking the massive, silent dam. We were all impatient and full of anticipation, each moment seemed like an eternity. Some began praying out loud, some tried to muffle their excitement by telling tales nobody cared to hear, others mumbled vague words, coughed, snorted, smoked, spat on the ground, and moved hither and thither. And when the cry arose: "There!," and the dam's gates slowly began rising and the water gushed out in a roar, a silence descended upon us, as if we were witnessing a miracle.

Describing this scene is beyond my powers, and even as I try to sketch this spectacle in writing my hand shivers. I have seen great dams and breathtaking waterfalls during my days on earth, but such an emotion has never captivated me quite like that. I was stunned and scared by the powerful torrent that resembled, in my eyes, a ferocious beast that had broken out of its cage. The lake by the dam filled up with incredible speed and water poured into the creek, washing along dry branches and various refuse in a terrible growl. Many went down to the creek to dip in the blessed water, others walked downstream back to town, singing and cheering like those taking a groom to their bride.

The water festivities lasted well into the night. Sheep were slaughtered and peasants sang and danced around the camp fires, a cloud of smoke hanging above their heads. No one stayed home that day. Muslims and Jews celebrated together and even though they didn't taste each other's foods, the joy was general and carried everyone along in a major celebration. I roamed around the merrymakers and hardly sat down with my family. Our gang of kids ran wild and the grown-ups didn't reprimand us and or try to quiet us down. Assad and Qassem were with me most of the time and as it got late, when I was most excited, I said what I did about wanting to be a peasant. Qassem silenced me with his embarrassing reply, while Assad—not interrupting the exchange—eyed me curiously as an uneasy smile spread across his face. We were close, Assad and I, in our thoughts, in our love for the city and its inhabitants, and in our effort to be involved with the life of the peasants. As for myself, I grumbled to him of the prohibitions my father had imposed on me, not to make friends with the sons of the peasants. When I was only five or six my father caused me one of the most humiliating disappointments of my life. I had come home glowing with joy, holding a wooden toy in the shape of a water pump, a

Shimon Ballas

present given to me by one of the Rashidiya students, and my father, in his commanding voice, demanded that I return the present and stop associating with students from that school. My tears didn't help, nor my mother's intervention, and I was forced to return the present, shamefaced.

I couldn't understand my father's behavior back then. He was one of the dignitaries, coming and going into Muslim homes, but in his own house he strictly maintained his unreasonable prohibitions. I was aggravated to be chained to these interdictions, and I only allowed myself to evade them when I'd grown up a bit, in spite of Reuben's supervision and snitching. A divided soul is the soul of a Jew, guarding uniqueness as it goes, zealous in faith and separation. In those days it was an accepted custom that business partnerships or friendships between a Jew and a Muslim did not take precedence over the taboo of eating the other's food or drinking from the other's vessels. Each was impure to the other and, on happy occasions, when Jews did sit in the company of Muslims, they didn't touch one another's food; if they wanted a sip of coffee, they'd take out cups brought from home. This custom was maintained at the riverside cafes as well, and no one regarded it as an unnatural phenomenon. Assad and I didn't abide by these prohibitions, secretly we would eat of the Muslims' foods we found palatable, and yet in their eyes we were unlike them, we didn't belong. Qassem made that much clear in his reply—he put me in my place, and it hurt. But even years later he still knew how to hurt me, always in his sharp and apparently neutral voice, which became slightly hoarse over time.

I didn't become a peasant, but the feelings that stirred my heart that night kept inciting me, and the time came when I realized the water festivities were, for me, sort of an oath taking ceremony, when I swore to be loyal and love my fellow citizens, and all who walk the homeland's soil. I can not remain unmoved when I recall those days. My native town was its own world, apart, alone on the bank of the Euphrates, far away from the new winds that had begun to blow in Baghdad. The town retained its way of life, integrating Bedouin pride with peasant humility. Flocks of sheep and camel caravans passed through its lanes, and sublime poetry lingered in its pure air. The Granary, people would call it; its soil was of pure gold, and the water of the Euphrates ran through its veins.

Today it is a city like any other, dressed up in modernity's robe, the glory of its past bundled up in the pulsing hearts of a generation gradually passing from this world.

IN AL-HILA WAS I delivered into life, on the second year of this century; I was the youngest son, after three daughters and a firstborn son, my senior by ten years. My father, Moshe Saussan, was an educated man, a graduate of the *Alliance* school in Baghdad, and ever since I can remember he was in charge of the properties of the wealthy Daniel family of Baghdad. Our family is one of the oldest in town, and according to one theory its origins lay in Persia, and its lineage goes back to the celebrated city of Shushan, the very Shushan that figures so prominently in the *Book of Esther*. At the age of four I was sent to a *Talmud Torah*, the only school for Jews at the time. The school consisted of four tiny rooms where students of various ages sat cramped next to each other on low benches. There was no blackboard, nor did we have any books, and the teacher would pass out large sheets of paper in a frame on which the letters of the Hebrew alphabet were printed, each line containing one letter with different vowel and vocalization marks. Each student was ordered to chant the letter with the right vocalization, and when he made a mistake the teacher's long stick would smack his fingertips. Except for the letters, we had to recite after the teacher verses of prayer whose meaning we couldn't understand. It was my good fortune to only attend this school for a year; it was closed when the *Alliance* opened, thanks to a donation from the Daniel family, and due to his function, my father was in charge of its administration. The teachers came from Baghdad and Constantinople and taught us French, Turkish, and Arabic. Religion classes were in the hands of rabbis, using methods no different than those practiced at the *Talmud Torah*. I was the youngest in class and one of the best students but my father never allowed me to go to bed at night before undergoing a demanding quiz that scared me more than any school exam. Over time, after he had realized that religion was outweighed by other subjects, he appointed a private tutor that showed up every afternoon to take away the best play time with kids in the neighborhood. The Hebrew teacher, replaced many times in accord with my progress, even came over to our house during the summer; because of this, I was probably the only kid in the neighborhood who never had a proper holiday throughout primary school. I hated those lessons and couldn't get myself at all interested in them. Even after I moved to Baghdad to continue my schooling at the *Alliance*, I made no effort to excel in my Hebrew classes. But years later, when I chose to study the history of religions, I appreciated those lessons because I could read and comprehend a Hebrew text without using translations.

My father's customs were contradictory. He used to wear traditional garb, a *keffiya* and *'aqal* on his head, and in the afternoon he used to sit with dignitaries in the cafe by the river bank smoking a nargileh. In Baghdad, where work sometimes kept him for days on end, he swapped his clothes for a European suit and replaced the *keffiya* and *'aqal* with a *sidara*. But just as he took great care not to differentiate himself in appearance from those around him, he went to great lengths to maintain a different way of life at home, different not only from Muslim homes, but also from the Jewish families in the neighborhood. We were the only children in the neighborhood, probably in the whole town as well, forced to eat with a fork and spoon and tie a napkin around our necks when we sat at the table. We were even forbidden to pick at rice and lentil dishes, like pilaf and *kushari*, which I loved dearly, and still do, with our fingers, like everyone else. Each morning before I left for school he'd check my clothes to make sure they were clean and then inspect my nails to make sure they were clipped properly. He imposed a strict disciplinary regime and it was only when he was away from home, when he stayed in Baghdad or Basra, that we gained any amount of freedom. My mother turned a blind eye to what we did and she let me and my sisters play and get our clothes dirty along with the other kids in the neighborhood. She wasn't strict about table manners either. Only from time to time she'd rebuke us, soft and forgiving: "Oh dear, if your father saw you now!"

Unlike my father, my mother hadn't studied at school and couldn't oversee our homework. She was born to a poor family with many children, and chosen by my father, many years her elder, thanks to her beauty. She admired my father and adapted to his regime at home; for her, he was not only husband and breadwinner, but the master whose instructions had to be obeyed. She was no different that way than most women in the neighborhood, yet she did not associate with them much, to keep my father's honor as the leader of the Jews. As I was the youngest child she gave me special treatment, and I always thought she loved me more than my siblings. I note this because I remember many occasions when my father was angry and wanted to punish me, and she rushed to my defense. One of his favorite punishments was a lock-up in the cellar. He never hit me, but he'd pull my ears and drag me down to the dark basement, full of blood-curdling creepers. I'd weep and cry out of fear and injured pride, and was overjoyed to see my mother come down to me, embrace me in her arms, and smuggle me into another room that served as a pantry, where she gave me sweets. Those moments with my mother were the happiest in my life— I'd cling to her, and sometimes doze off in her lap.

And just as I was under my mother's warm protection, Reuben was my father's protege, training to be his right-hand man in business. From the day Reuben became an adult, after a Bar-Mitzvah ceremony at the synagogue, my father began taking him to his office and teaching him book keeping. I don't remember that time at all, for I was only two years old; the only thing I do remember is that Reuben was always trying to imitate my father's ways, and being the eldest he assumed authority when my father was away. His main concern was to make sure I didn't go out after school and play outside the neighborhood with Muslim kids. My mother didn't interfere and gave free reign to his blatant arrogance toward me and my sisters, but when he'd inform on me to my father she looked annoyed and sometimes reprimanded him. There was always tension between him and me; he harbored a certain animosity toward me which he never tried to conceal, and after my father died, circumstances provided him with pretexts to deepen it.

I have no wish to seek the causes for my brother's behavior. I am telling of my father, and if I mention Reuben, I do so only to point out some traits he inherited from him. The zeal for tribal tradition was one, but whereas my father was graced with wisdom and a noble spirit, Reuben's zeal was callous and insensitive, and over time it came to dominate his personality. My father was the product of his times, and contradictory values were in conflict in his world. His education had prepared him to be open to western culture, but circumstances didn't allow him to revise the value system on which he was raised. The text books at the *Alliance* introduced him to Europe, its history and its ways, and some time before the Great War he even visited England and France, but the Western world remained foreign to him, a world from which some useful things might be gleaned but which could not, in any way, be fully accepted or made part of oneself. Unlike Egypt and Lebanon, Iraq in those days was closed off to western influence and was not in touch with Europe, except for commercial ties, until the Great War. As a Jew living in a traditional, mostly Shi'ite, environment he was in a state of double protection, both from his Muslim milieu and from the fashionable heresies circulating among educated Jews, *Alliance* graduates in particular. Many contradictions existed in my father, and I must say that thanks to these contradictions he did not impress us as a tyrant in spite of the harsh discipline he practiced at home. He did not interfere with household affairs and I can not remember hearing him rebuke my mother or raise his voice at her even once. I was annoyed by his rule forbidding me to associate with the peasant kids but when I was nine he already allowed me to ride his noble mare, seeing how I was attached to it and how I took care of it. Riding was my favorite hobby and the mare accepted all my whims with forbearance. In fact, riding has been a hobby of mine throughout my life and, to this day, I never miss an opportunity to mount a good horse.

The more I try to depict my father's character, the more I come up short. In truth, I didn't know him well at all. He wasn't intimate with us; he didn't tell us stories or play with us like fathers do with their children, and he refrained from talking about himself or the problems he faced in business in our presence. The little I know of him I learned from my mother, who was also cautious not to reveal what she knew. He was the utmost authority, to be respected. We kissed his hand on Friday night after *kiddush*, the blessings over wine, and asked his permission for anything that required permission. We were examined by him and it was at his hands that we risked chastisement or punishment. Apart from my mother, with whom he'd talk quietly in their room, only Reuben got to know him up close, while my sisters and I were never allowed a glimpse into his world. He wasn't particularly interested in me and was satisfied that I did as he said and excelled as a student. His many business affairs, as well as political events on the eve of the World War and during that war compelled him to spend the major part of the day away from home, and I was somehow left alone to do as I pleased. In those days the Turkish governor became more severe toward the inhabitants and brutally suppressed the uprising in the Middle Euphrates district. The leaders of the uprising were hanged in public and the governor's cronies, conspiring to divide the population, spread rumors that blamed the Jews for the disruption of peaceful life. Two Jews were murdered and Jewish owned shops were looted or set on fire. Times were hard until the English came, and my father was busy working and left the house in my mother's hands. I was the sole beneficiary from this slackening of discipline, since my brother was constantly at my father's side and couldn't keep an eye on me.

The arrival of the English and the dismantling of Turkish rule was a relief for the Jews. Business was booming and many young Jews, especially graduates of *Alliance*, found work as clerks and translators in the new institutions. The Jews never concealed their support of the British, served them loyally, and even pulled strings to prevent the establishment of a national government, but the British didn't follow their suggestions. When the time came they crowned Faisal and cancelled the mandate. My father, who found a willingness among the new rulers to bring some of the modern world's accomplishments to Iraq, managed to acquire a franchise to run an electric power station, and thus his name was forever bound with the age of electricity that graced the city. That private station kept operating until 1936 when it was nationalized and connected to the national power grid. My father was a man of many talents, and in these pages I am fulfilling the duty of a son who respected him deeply, though I have been unable to delve too far into the contradictions that existed in him. I should also mention that he deserves my praises for sending me to live with his brother in Baghdad to continue my studies, and later encouraging me to go to Beirut. In Baghdad I lived in my uncle's house in the Takht-al-Takiah neighborhood, and on every visit he used to seat me next to him and check the progress of my studies. I was sure that he found this gratifying, but he never revealed it to me. He always instilled the feeling in me that I was under examination and would have to pass further exams. He was seventy at the time, by my calculation, agile and of sound constitution, until he was afflicted by a virulent illness whose nature we did not know. He became horribly emaciated and was soon unable to take care of business. The doctors were at a loss and when I left for Beirut he was preparing to go to India for treatment. A telegram from Reuben broke the news of his death to me. He died on the ship, a few hours before it arrived in the port of Bombay. On his own, far away from home and family, he was buried in foreign soil instead of the land on which he was raised and to which he remained loyal throughout his life.

I wrote of my father while bringing up childhood memories because this childhood passed in his presence and was marked by the formidable impression he made. I can't talk about my childhood without being moved—I had a happy childhood, nourished by the softness of the soil and the scent of hay, the murmur of the water of the Euphrates and the singing of Bedouin on moonlit nights and stormy days. al-Hila, for me, is the horse, the cow, the goat, and every four-legged creature and bird; it is the narrow alleys and the open fields, the peasant's sweat and the clicking plough; it's the nightly conversation by a lantern, and the fairy tale journey to enchanted worlds. How could I not be moved when I evoke those days, and now I find Assad's voice here full of yearning—even after the bitter disappointments the changing times brought upon him, even after the uprooting and settlement in what he saw fit to call "the land of promise," he had only the most sublime words to describe his native town. Indeed, al-Hila is not just a place to be born and die in, it is much more, it is an ever-lasting belonging.

IN APRIL, 1969 I saw Assad Nissim for the last time. He had become the object of attention as a guest at the reception in the presidential palace for participants in the Arab Writers Conference, where he was a member of the Iraqi delegation. On entering the crowded air-conditioned hall, I found him talking with a group of authors, tele-vision cameras following his every move. He seemed at ease, pleased with the gestures of respect showered upon him by directives from the top, but when he was called to the stage to speak he could barely conceal his excitement and his voice trembled. He read a passage from an old poem, and I examined his full, Mongolian face thinking that without the gray strands in his black, straight hair, the taut skin of his face would not have revealed his age.

Afters years of neglect, Assad had been rejuvenated, but it happened right when the handful of Jews who chose to stay in Iraq after the massive emigration were not so fortunate. A poem of eight lines only, published on the front page of *al-Jumhuriya*, and titled "A Jew in the Shade of Islam," put him in the limelight. As if by magic he became one of the most photographed figures in the papers and on television. Quick-penned reporters rushed to adorn him with superlatives and elaborately praise his literary work, as well as his personality—a model Iraqi patriot. Much hypocrisy was involved, but those who knew Assad can testify that in those eight lines he succinctly expressed not only his own truth, but also the dilemma he found himself in the middle of throughout his life. This is what he wrote:

> If the religion of Moses is my vessel of faith
> the shade of Muhammad's Law is my home
>
> The tolerance of Islam is what I lean upon
> And the Koranic tongue my verse's treasure chest
>
> Safe-keeps the love I owe Muhammad's people
> And though it is to Moses my prayers go
>
> It is the loyalty of Samawal I cannot forego
> As I rejoice in Baghdad or let my misery grow

After the poem was published I told Kazem: "This is Assad, that's the way he was when I met him, and that's the way he remains."

"It's time you two made peace with each other," he told me.

"There was never a quarrel, we just parted ways."

"All the more so, I'm certain he'd be delighted if you call him."

I didn't call. But at the reception, after he read the poem, I was going to step up to him to shake his hand, but an Egyptian journalist stopped me: "I'm told that you and Assad Nissim grew up in the same town, could you tell me something about him?" It was evident from the way the question was phrased that he knew nothing about me, and someone had probably turned him to me in order to get rid of him. I could have avoided him and been on my way, but I told him that al-Hila was a small town in those days and everyone knew each other, a response that brought about even more questions which I had to answer with few words and demonstrable unwillingness. After I finally got rid of him I regretted ever having responded, and grew worried that he might work my name into his story in order to add sensational note. But he was one of those ignorant journalists, most Egyptian journalists are, who don't bother to inform themselves of the person they interview either before or after they talk to them. He had no idea who I was and didn't ask about me; neither, it appears, did he find in my answers anything that might inflate his story, and therefore he left me out. Indeed, some good can come of stupidity. But I owe him doubly, for it was careless of me to approach Assad in front of the cameras and draw to him the kind of attention that I do not at all care for.

I never saw Assad again with my own eyes but I followed his appearances on television and kept everything he published or that was written about him in the papers. Two years later he became the center of public attention again when he suffered a heart attack and President al-Bakr dispatched his adjutant general to his bed at Fayiddi hospital carrying flowers. Then I was given another opportunity, a last chance, to convey my affection and wish for his recovery from the bottom of my heart, but I didn't, and I regret it. Two months after he was released from the hospital, he and his wife were given a passport and he flew to Beirut; from there, they went on to Europe, and then Tel Aviv.

The story of our relationship is convoluted and took many turns, just as our paths in life since those faraway days till now, as we both find ourselves reaching our eighties. We've had a difficult dispute and the rift has persisted for some fifty years but I never made our disagreement public and never mentioned his name in any of my articles or lectures. He has done the same, to the best of my knowledge, to this very day. God favored me in that I was in the United States when the stunning news of his defection was published, and that saved me from journalists seeking a response and a condemnation. What I do have to say about Assad I'd rather say in my own way, not through interviews and declarations to the media. These pages of memories will tell the story of a friendship, they are the written testimony about me and my era, and it's all the same to me if they should displease close friends and distant acquaintances, for these pages will not see the light of day while I am alive.

IT'S BEEN SEVERAL WEEKS that I haven't visited the home of Jawad al-'Alawi on the usual Thursday, and he expressed his astonishment about it at the recent Academy board meeting. I promised to go, and so I went. I met Moustafa al-Sharbati, a regular guest these days, and Munir Sarqis, the Defense Ministry's chief translator. There was also a young man in a tailored suit, presented to me as Khaled, a lawyer working at the Attorney General's office. They were arguing over the lack of coordination among the academies of the Arabic language in Arab countries to determine parallels for technical and scientific terms and, naturally, I was asked for my opinion on the subject. From what I managed to hear I gathered that Munir had instigated the discussion while Moustafa tried to defend the work of the Academy and its coordination with sister academies. Munir was right, and if I didn't have to be careful not to cause Moustafa any further discomfort—since he was already hurt by the Minister's decision to choose me to chair the preparatory committee of the festivities—I'd have had no qualms about voicing my criticism of the anarchy that reigns in the field. I took a stance that would satisfy them both. Without dismissing Munir's argument, I blamed the academies in Syria and Egypt for a lack of serious commitment to collaboration, a claim not devoid of truth, although we too, and Moustafa personally, being the secretary, had done little to improve our ties. As a matter of fact, the relations among the academies were not marked by collaboration, but by rampant competition based on condescension and utter disregard.

Yet Munir, rather than criticize the lack of collaboration among the academies, focused his attack on the nomination system for members of the Academy, which favored well known writers and university professors while ignoring those who work in the field on a daily basis as translators, journalists, workers in research institutes, etc. . . Those who face problems and have to come up with immediate solutions are not asked for their opinion, but their solutions are usually accepted and become prevalent, until the Academy members find the time to discuss them. The most ridiculous, he added, are the Academy's rejection announcements and the alternatives it proposes, to which no one pays any attention. He was relentless in asserting his view, to the point of exaggeration, but that's how things were. Untalented and lazy people like Moustafa and his ilk are ensconced in the Academy while a clever guy like Munir remains out of it.

Jawad heard him out with a forgiving smile but when Moustafa responded, saying that this was an insult to members of the Academy, he quickly remarked that not every criticism should be taken as an insult, and it was our duty to initiate such criticism and take it into consideration. Before Moustafa could respond, he put an end to the argument by saying: "What concerns me is the Iranian problem," shifting the conversation to a topic, the subversive activities of Iranian exiles, that was constantly in the headlines. He asked the young lawyer if the government intended to bring inflammatory leaders to trial but Moustafa wouldn't even let him reply before expressing his astonishment at how Khomeini was allowed to act freely without being reminded of his place as an exile, forbidden to engage in political activity. Khaled said the matter was not as simple as it appeared, because Iraq had not provided a refuge to Khomeini and company out of pure hospitality, but also because we supported his struggle against the Shah. His reply didn't satisfy Moustafa, who argued that struggling against the Shah wasn't the same as working to establish a Shi'ite party in Iraq. Jawad concurred, and said Khomeini was meddling in Iraq's internal affairs and inciting a war between religious factions.

I listened to them and thought of Zuhair, of whom we had no news since he'd been arrested. I cautiously asked to hear about the fate of the detainees but Khaled had nothing to say and probably refrained from revealing anything or speaking his mind. He began to look uncomfortable, until he finally got up to part with us. At that very moment Aziz Laham appeared at the door, so we found ourselves saying good bye to one and greeting another.

Aziz Laham's entrance interrupted the conversation for a little while, especially since he was noticeably drunk. He chose to sit on a chair next to the door, in spite of Jawad's entreaties to seat him on the large couch, next to Moustafa. His eyes were bloodshot and swollen, a thick cigar between his fingers, and he sat upright with his legs apart, as if he was going to leave any second. His expression was mute and as our conversation got underway again he just sat there listening, his gaze mindlessly fleeting over our faces. A robust man, tall and ponderous, there was something pathetic about him, maybe because he always dyed his hair and wore a suit and tie, even on the hottest days. It's not merely that he was still trying to appear the dandy in late middle age, I thought, but also to compensate for the shame that has haunted him since he was released from prison. Don't judge a man until you find yourself in his place, I thought, and I couldn't help myself from wondering about his faint heart and how, with a body like that, he could possibly have withstood torture. I thought of Qassem, at whose office I met Laham for the first time, some forty years ago. He was a young lawyer then, and a party activist, just like Qassem, but what a difference between the two! This plunged me right back into worrying about Zuhair, now going through the hell of interrogation, and there would be no telling whether he'd come out of it a ruin or not. Just then I heard 'Aziz in his thick, tough voice: "You can say things at home you can't say in cafes."

We all turned toward him, and I was surprised to find his eyes focused on mine, as if asking for my response. "And what is said in the cafes?" I asked innocently.

His lips shaped into a thin smile and he kept eyeing me without replying. I couldn't figure out where he was taking this, and on account of the silence that enveloped the room I added that it had been years since I sat in a cafe. "You know how to watch out for yourself," he snapped, emitting a forced, unpleasant laugh.

I was a little late in coming to realize that his words were aimed at me from the start and instead of ignoring what he said, I helped him out. I could have answered bluntly to throw him off balance, but I didn't want to spoil the atmosphere and embarrass Jawad since Aziz was his guest. Moustafa came to my rescue, in a soothing voice: "God have mercy on your father, who doesn't watch out for himself these days?" And Jawad added: "We're among friends, we talk openly."

"But you don't know what the people say and feel. Step out of your shell for a second!"

"The people unite around the President," Moustafa pronounced.

Aziz gave him a mocking stare and said nothing.

"People like to exaggerate," Jawad concluded. "There won't be an ethnic rebellion in Iraq. The Shi'ites are not discriminated against here as they are in Lebanon, and if Khomeini is popular, it's for being an Imam, not a rebel leader."

Again Aziz said nothing and it seemed as though his provocative comment was nothing more than that, the words of a frustrated drunkard who'd do anything to draw some attention. Yet he kept staring at me in a way that started to get on my nerves and soon he muttered: "A man who watches out for himself speaks ambiguously, so as not to get caught saying anything incriminating."

I wasn't sure if he insisted on aiming his words at me out of a desire to challenge me or was trying to get me to concur with him that we were salon philosophers, removed from the people. Either way, I wanted to know what he saw in me that so displeased him, but his words went by with no comment, and at that point the appearance of the helper who came to serve coffee stopped the conversation. We didn't pick up our discussion of the Iranians. Aziz stayed out of it, and went on smoking his cigar in a mock display of condescension.

My suspicions were verified when I got up to leave. He shook my hand feebly, as if forced to, and menacingly said: "We'll talk again."

"Have we anything else to do?" chuckled Jawad.

"The Doctor does," he pointed at me.

"You wish to talk to me?" I asked.

"He wrote a book calling for a jihad against the Jews!" he added, ignoring my question, and let out a rude, disgusting laugh.

"You're drunk," I told him, overcoming my rage.

Moustafa pulled him to the couch, and he let himself be dragged, laughing and waving his hand.

Jawad saw me out.

"He kept trying to provoke me," I said.

"A miserable man, don't take it to heart," he replied.

Miserable, but not without malice. I wonder what else he said after I left. Jawad wouldn't tell me, and I couldn't rely on Moustafa. A sycophant like him would try to prove he defended me. Did I need to be defended? Jihad against the Jews! What on earth was eating him?

Had I reacted immediately he wouldn't have continued his provocation. Watch out for myself? Speak ambiguously? How dare he? That's begging for an answer that would put him to shame. Or does the wet man feel no fear of rain? He doesn't mind being reminded of his sin, wearing the mark of his disgrace with pride. A traitor to his party, contemptuous to a wife who threw him out of the house but embraced by the government for having publicly renounced Communism! A wretched soul. It goes without saying that I shouldn't pay him any heed, but what he said to my face—and anything else he might have mentioned—others must also be saying, perhaps behind my back. Whispering, trying to guess at my intentions, I've known this all along and should have no reason to be surprised.

Too bad Kazem wasn't there. I called to tell him and his daughter said he had caught a cold, and was in bed with a fever. I'll visit tomorrow.

IT LOOKS LIKE KHOMEINI will be deported soon. He's been accused of subversive activity against the regime in Iran, something Iraq can not afford in view of the Friendship Accord and the good-neighbor relations between the countries. The allegation is weird and ridiculous. Is it our job to stop the Shah's regime from collapsing? Who would believe our laughable motive for deporting him? Kazem isn't at all surprised at the government's trick for getting rid of the man and his supporters. The deportation will show the world that Iraq has no part in the growing resistance movement in Iran, and save us from international complications and pressure from the Americans. Still, he can't conceal his disappointment, and his fear that this step might exacerbate ethnic tensions.

I found him lying in bed, feeble, and coughing violently. The doctors ordered total rest, and his elder daughter told me the cough was cause for concern since he once had TB. His daughters take turns by his bedside and the grandchildren keep quiet so as not to disturb his rest. I didn't tell him about Aziz Laham, and left for home after just half an hour.

I hope to find him better tomorrow and able to share the thoughts rumbling in my head. I have no doubt that we are on the verge of a new era and should we fail to prepare ourselves, we may well end up immersed in bloody ethnic conflicts. Kazem's sympathy lies with the D'awa people, which is understandable, but this party, in spite of its popular nature and the just demands it makes, does not promote Muslim unity, it enhances Shi'ite separatism. His consistent rejection of any separatist tendency doesn't contradict his basic sympathy for the disenfranchised, and he believes the struggle for equality will remove the obstacles to unity. This makes sense, but has its dangers. That's what I wrote about in the introduction to *The Jews in History*, and he agreed with my every word. Not a jihad against the Jews, as in Aziz Laham's hostile interpretation, but a platform for a comprehensive campaign against Zionism and western dominance. I said we are in need of an *Islamic Manifesto*, similar to the bankrupt *Communist Manifesto*. I talked of a general Muslim unity for a social and cultural revolution that could pull us away from dependence on the west and prepare us to construct a just society, a shining model for the entire world. Aziz Laham's feeble mind could not have grasped this, nor was it his desire. But I fear that many are just as mindless, and would interpret my words in the same vein. I've always had a problem with such people, people who don't understand me or, worse, understand just a little and distort my intentions. I have difficulty communicating, I realize that, but I think I'm entitled to expect some effort, some genuine willingness to understand.

Kazem was so right when he told me, in that first meeting in Beirut, that we complement each other in our thoughts, him on the inside, and me on the outside. Indeed, things have remained like that to this day. He is planted on the inside, wise and emotional, and I'm outside, on the threshold, on the border between acceptance and rejection. Desire for extremism is a malignant trait, delineating sharp distinctions between for and against, between light and darkness, with us or with our adversaries. Thus ideologies were created, in whose name peoples fought, built empires and brought them down. I am not an ideological man, I am the creature of the time between the two wars, the most turbulent period in the twentieth century, an era that changed the face of the earth, the high tide of ideologies — Communism, Fascism, and Nazism. Europe was wild with excitement, fomenting war, and in our region colonial rule was consolidated and Zionism established itself, like a dagger in the heart of Arab soil. On coming back from America, after completing my studies, I spent two months in Europe and witnessed the public confusion, the lack of perspective, people's immersion in the mundane, their supposed yearning for stability. The Great War had uprooted terms that grew out of the past century. The twentieth century began, in actuality, in 1914, in the war that ushered in the new era, the age of the tank, the airplane, and sophisticated lethal weapons, the age of technology and social shock.

I could sense this turn in the ways of man in Europe more than in America. Europe emerged broken from the war, licking its wounds, and the average citizen, whether liberal or socialist, catholic or atheist, laborer or intellectual, looked like he had no goal except an easier, more comfortable life. Worship of material progress took the place of religious worship and was manifested in the unrestrained admiration for great factories, for research institutes and universities, for movie theaters and dance halls, for the automobile, the airplane, the tram and the metro, for all the technological achievements that almost entirely erased that not at all distant world of yesterday from memory. This citizen had new heroes whose photos and actions filled the newspapers: bankers and politicians, movie actors and industrial magnates, pilots, generals, and athletes. This citizen clung to what the present had to offer, and turned his back on the values that he was brought up with in school. And I, having just emerged from among the books, found myself wondering: is this the only path, in the age of science and technology? Is man doomed to shed the ideals of the spirit [like old skin] and join the rat race? And what was a man of the East like me to make of all this?

After more than six years of study in America, the tour in Europe reinforced my conviction regarding Islam's supremacy over Christianity. For while Christianity made do with spiritual preaching, and instructed believers to say 'Let Cæsar have his due', Islam was founded on the unity of believers, regardless of race and language, on faith in one god. This unity prevented the growth of a clerical power next to the government, as in the case of the church in Christianity and the priesthood in Judaism; on the other hand, Islam endowed men of religion with the authority to create legislation in the spirit of Islamic principles, which condemn tyranny and social injustice, and are based on care for the general good, without depriving the individual. The laws of Islam, even if they were partly rigid and arbitrary, were fundamentally open to social change and therefore did not pose an obstacle to progress or create a divide between faith and a changing reality. Europe needed centuries to liberate itself from the tyranny of the church and only after successfully separating the church from the state did it embark upon the high road for the new age of modernity and individual liberty. But this democracy proved false as well, leaving the individual at the mercy of an authority that was no longer in the hands of a king or a tyrant, but the hands of financial barons and politicians. Worst of all—this democracy divided people internally and left the individual with no faith.

In the midst of confusion in Europe many voiced disgust with Western materialism and praised Eastern spirituality; these were faint echoes of the Orientalist school of the last century—they got no attention and were muffled by the turmoil. I felt no sympathy for them because they spoke out of distress, not honest faith, and their self-righteous preaching was heavily tainted by condescension towards the Orient, in the guise of a longing for primitive simplicity. The Orientalist school revealed itself soon enough as an extension of colonialism and every time I heard such talk of going back to the sources, to the wide expanses of prophecy and so on, I was offended and angered. It was a celebration of hypocrisy, especially since—between the lines—it insinuated an animosity toward Islam as a fanatical and tyrannic religion. I saw fit to respond to these falsifications in a letter to the *Times of London*, in which I wrote that an immense civilization flourished under Islam while Europe lay in the obscurity of the dark ages, under the tyranny of the church and its greedy rulers. I added that the chance to break free of the Eastern peoples' backwardness is not to be found in denial of Islam nor in imitation of the West, but in maintaining their authentic identity as members of a different civilization, an essentially Muslim civilization which may, in time, take on some traits of western civilization, which is Christian. But the *Times*, supposedly a standard bearer of the freedom of speech, omitted the last, most important passage of my letter, probably considering this more than a "native" could say!

I was twenty eight when I wrote it, I wrote it as a Jew, and as a Jew I revised and elaborated on it in an article that was published by *al-Ahrar*, a paper in Beirut. I had stopped there, for three weeks, on my way to Baghdad. I still have a copy—it came out on August 28, 1930, and anyone wanting to check if my views have changed since then can look it up. I articulated an honest call to all Jews in the Arab East to emerge from their separatism and join shoulders with their Muslim and Christian brethren against Zionism. Jihad against the Jews? Only a mean, disfigured spirit could interpret my book that way. Not against them, but for their own good as human beings, I believed, and still do, that it was their duty to break free of the tribal concept, to shake off the ethnocentric and xenophobic mentality that characterizes Judaism, the same mentality that finds its vulgar and brutal expression in Zionism.

DURING MY SECOND VISIT in America, in April 1936, two months after my mother's death, I asked Jane if she remembered her response when I told her, in Beirut, that I had intended to convert to Islam so I could marry her, and she said: "It seems so long ago, now."

"And now, would you respond differently?" I asked.

"I don't know. Maybe."

"You were angry with me for not telling you before the wedding."

"Because you didn't share your thoughts with me."

"Not only that. You also said it might have been a good solution for both of us."

She was silent for a moment, then said: "But another solution was found."

The solution was fifteen pounds in gold, hush-money for the rabbi. We were put in a frustrating position, told only after our wedding at the American consulate that Syrian law did not recognize civil marriage and we had to remarry in a religious ceremony according to the religion to which the husband belongs. It was hard for me to put up with, and I seriously considered converting to Islam, to save Jane the long and humiliating conversion procedures.

But some Jewish acquaintances I consulted suggested that I take the usual path and directed me to an ancient rabbi who asked no questions. He'd have sold his god for gold!

Jane had changed. The two years that passed since my last visit carried her a long way from that fleeting episode; she was already immersed in her world, working in her father's office and raising Jamil as a real American. What good were my attempts to evoke her memory or share my thoughts? Of what I had intended to tell her I wrote later, in a letter from Cairo, and she didn't reply. It was only after my second letter that she sent a short sharp answer: For me you will remain Jimmy's father. Indeed, that is what I remained, and every year or two she'd send me his photo.

It was a last visit, that visit before the divorce, even though I still believed we would live together again. Her father was cold toward me, but reminded me more than once that my place with the architectural firm in Boston was still reserved for me. He had already stopped believing I'd come, and I gave no indication I might change my mind. Jamil was four years old, a blue eyed boy with blond curly hair. On the first day he hesitated before approaching me, but quickly grew accustomed to calling me 'Daddy' and sitting in my lap. I saw him again twelve years later, in the summer of 1948, when he was already sixteen and a tall, handsome youth. "Meet Daddy," Jane told him, and I stood there, my legs trembling.

Jamil was her consolation. Hers, and her parents'. She looked down when I said so, and got busy with the folds of her dress. Thin wrinkles had appeared in the corners of her eyes, and her brown hair was trimmed to shoulder length. She was still pretty and attractive, but had accepted her fate and built her life around her son and her work. We didn't get much of a chance to talk and even when we were alone we were silent more than we spoke. We were like strangers, after such a long separation, but during those moments in her company I felt that such a profound understanding existed between us that talking was unnecessary. At times I lost my sense of reality and it seemed to me that we had never separated, that all the years that passed and all that had happened to her and to me was only a dream. What bars us from a fresh start, I asked myself? What does time matter when the feeling is the same. Such ethereal notions swept through my mind, leaving a heavy depression behind.

I am sure that Jane too was visited by such thoughts. She didn't have an easy life, and I imagine that to herself she too must have said it all happened by mistake. Hers? Mine? I don't know. At this very moment, as I put this down, I can say with certainty that my life would have been happier had she consented to come back to Baghdad with me. Could my life have been happy if I had agreed to stay in America? I think not, but I shall not hide this under my tongue, I will admit that on that visit in 1936 I had reason to believe we would live together again. I had my hopes up based on a promise that I'd be posted to a diplomatic position at the Embassy in Washington but this did not come about, and the years went by.

After our divorce Jane kept dispatching letters regularly, and I kept her posted with my news. Just before the war broke out she announced she was about to marry a pilot, without mentioning that he was serving in the American air force. Her letters became less frequent then, and I prayed against a disaster. But a disaster took place, in 1944, in Normandy. Two marriages, two tragedies in her young life! Jamil is your consolation, I told her, and she remained silent. And to Jamil I said: I have no right to tell you what to do, but I have one wish to make: don't do anything that might upset your mother. My fear that he would reject me and bear a grudge against me proved false. He found ample time to talk to me about his future, his mind was already made up to study electrical engineering. On the day I parted he asked me when he could see his younger sister. I deferred to his mother and said he could, the moment his mother permitted. But the visit didn't take place. It was postponed twice for trivial reasons and the meeting with Butheina only occurred some ten years later, when Jane was no longer alive.

I stood weeping by Jane's grave. Both my children held me on either side, the aging parents sobbing behind us. Thus, the siblings met by Jane's grave, and I, the father, wished the earth to open and offer me rest by the side of the dear woman I loved.

JANE HAD GREAT AFFECTION for Assad Nissim. She always asked about him and sent her regards. When I visited in 1936 I told her about the argument he and I had a short while before my departure, following an article I published in support of pre-military education in the schools. I didn't linger on the details, but conveyed the thrust of my article and Assad's argument against me.

She listened silently, and then said: "Assad is a clever guy." I told her I knew she would side with him, and she smiled: "On this issue I definitely disagree with you."

This was an issue we disagreed on just as we were getting to know each other. She was a student in the department of Semitic languages referred to me by one of her professors to help her unravel the mysteries of Arabic grammar. She was five years younger than me, and I was about to complete my doctoral dissertation on British diplomacy in the Middle East after the opening of the Suez canal. She told me her choice of discipline was inspired by her high school theology teacher, who had taught her to love the languages spoken by Jesus and the apostles. She had a slim figure, blue eyes, and small tender hands that I longed to hold in mine. We sat in the cafeteria and I noticed the inquisitive looks other students gave us, some of them were unable to restrain themselves from approaching her to ask something as they looked through me. I was shy and had always believed there was nothing about me to attract the girls, especially as there were only a few of them, followed by innumerable suitors. I diverted my energies to sports and managed to stand out as one of the best tennis players on the Humanities team. Still, a popular good looking girl like Jane, would it have occurred to her to sit with me in the cafeteria if she weren't in need of my help? For her, I thought, I was one of those people that could be gotten in touch with as needed and forgotten about later. I was aggravated by the understanding smile she gave those spies that stepped up to her, as if telling them "You have nothing to worry about, I'm just studying." On our first meeting I decided to terminate the ungrateful role she had assigned me. I showed her my picture in an officer's uniform of the American Army, and she let out a cry of surprise: "It's you!" She looked at me, then back at the picture, several times: "It's hard for me to imagine you as a military man!"

I told her about my two years at the engineering school that was associated with the Defense Department, where students get military training and at the end of four years, are given an officer's rank. "I was forced to leave that school," I said, "to specialize in civil engineering, so I was prevented from getting the rank."

"And you regret it?"

"Yes," I replied. "I can't say I care for the honor of being an officer in the American army, but I regret the training I missed."

"You're so not like this!" She laughed, and put the photo down on the table.

"The uniform doesn't become me?"

"On the contrary, but you don't look. . . like you!"

"I chose the cavalry," I told her. "Riding is my great passion since I was a child. I was very happy at that school."

"It shows." She picked up the photo again, "You have a challenging look, I'd even say vain." She laughed again.

"I think military training should be imposed in all universities," I said, putting the photo back in my pocket. "It's the best way to educate, to discipline, to build character, and to develop a sense of responsibility."

"I didn't expect to hear such things from you."

"What did you expect?"

She turned her head and didn't reply. I went on discussing the merits of military training and said it would even be good to impose it on high school students.

"If you brought up this idea at a student meeting nobody would support you," she said.

"And you'd stand up and speak against me?"

"I'm not one of those who speak in meetings, but I absolutely disagree. They're opposites. Military training and studies don't go hand in hand."

Two opposites. That's what perplexed her, that these two opposites should exist in me. A diligent student, thin, bespectacled, of medium height, suddenly there he was in an officer's uniform, preaching militarism! I managed to arouse her curiosity, and from that day on I was no longer just the Arabic grammar teacher.

Assad had different reasons. What troubled him in my article was the passage regarding Jewish schools. "You're playing with fire," he defied me. "Who are you trying to please?"

I had indeed known the community institutions wouldn't let my words pass without comment, particularly since the timing of its publication was unfortunate, but I did not expect the first response to come from Assad, and with such severity. He came into my office at City Hall unexpectedly, holding the paper in his hand, and before I had time to get up to greet him he unleashed his allegations at me. "You distrust me?" I asked in astonishment.

"I want to know what made you write an article like this at just this time!"

"What makes a person write an article?" I asked again. "If you don't like it, that's a question of opinion."

"Well then, I don't trust your opinion," he angrily dropped the paper on my desk.

I decided to let it pass. I could have told him that the date of publication was the editor's decision, after postponing it for two entire weeks, but clinging to this did not seem right; besides, he could have replied that it was my duty to prevent publication in light of the tragic events that had taken place in the mean time. Two Jews were murdered during those two weeks, and Assad himself was very tense after an attempt was made on the life of the secretary of the Zawaraa club, of which he was a founding member. I held both his arms and asked him to sit down. "If you're angry with me, I accept your anger with love, just let us speak quietly."

I called the attendant to serve us tea and closed the door. Assad told me he had learned of the article's publication from the President of the Community, who called him at the editorial office. "The papers are brimming with anti-Jewish incitement," he went on in the same aggressive tone. "They print elegies for the Hitler Youth, and you picked just now to blame the Jews for shirking their military service?"

"That's not what I wrote."

"Haroun!" He slapped his hand on the table, "Why don't you tell me what made you write this article?"

"Let's be frank," I said, pulling a chair to sit next to him.

"That's precisely what I want, for you to be frank and tell me why now, when *al-'Alam al-'Arabi* publishes *Mein Kampf* with great pomp and circumstance, when *al-Yaqda* won't leave the Jewish question alone, when the Jews are accused of Zionist propaganda, what made you add your voice to theirs just now?"

"You won't let me speak."

"Speak, speak, that's what I came here for," he said, raising both his hands, but before I could utter a word he went on: "You know what they demand of us? Of me, of all the community dignitaries? To publish a declaration of patriotism, to swear that we are loyal to Iraq and reject Zionism! Instead of silencing the inciters, we are required to prove our loyalty!"

He looked at me with burning eyes. I had never seen him so upset, and for a moment I felt a pang of guilt for having unintentionally added to his distress. A celebrated poet who appears in crowded popular gatherings in the mosques, author of the moving poem about 'Abd al-Mun'im al-Sa'adun, editor of a literary review whose attention is sought by the best writers — they're asking for declarations of loyalty from a man like him?

The attendant knocked on the door and served us tea, and when he left I said: "You are a dear man, Assad, you are respected and admired."

He stirred his tea without replying. I went on in the same vein and added that I too would feel offended if a man like him made such a declaration.

"The insult has already been inflicted," he replied. "The demand came from the Prime Minister's office."

"You see?" I clung to his answer, "that is the motive for writing the article!"

He looked at me as though not following. I told him the insult was in the system, but the blame can not be placed on one side only. The government requires declarations of loyalty to calm things down, and the community leaders think they fulfill their obligation with verbal gestures, and sometimes by donating money. Both seem satisfied to extinguish local fires without trying to locate the source of the fire and eliminate it. This faulty system has been invalidated, I told him, it belongs to a different era, when Jews and Christians were considered protected subjects, exempt from the duty of jihad, but liable to pay taxes and take loyalty oaths. I added that I didn't blame the Jews for shirking their military service, but criticized the Service Indemnity Bill, that I was demanding a universal draft, for rich and poor, Muslims, Jews and Christians.

"Your attack was against the Jews, that even the poor among them are helped by the community to pay the indemnity and not serve."

"Isn't it true?"

"These days?"

"These days too."

"It's useless to argue with you," he said and stood up.

"That's because in your heart you agree with me," I insisted.

"I don't agree with any criticism that aids the inciters."

"The criticism was only a small passage, it wasn't the topic of the article."

"Hitler and Mussolini's admirers were there before you on the topic of pre-military education," he replied, with hostility and disdain.

I didn't respond. At that moment I also felt there was no point in arguing any further. But Assad had another point to make, and he coldly added: "If there is still one thing to connect us, it is rage at Reuben who brought you to this condition. You want to humiliate the community leaders at any cost, and you don't care if you denigrate an entire public, your own people!"

"That has nothing to do with it," I objected, "I wrote as a Jew."

"As a Jew from without," he said with a bitter smile, and turned to go.

I AM MAKING EVERY effort to tell of things as they happened but memory betrays me and many events seem detached from the context of that time, leaving me with disturbing question marks. '35 and '36 were decisive years in my life, and the dispute with Assad over my article was only a way station on the route that led to the break between us. I met with him often. I also met with Qassem, at the offices of *Al-Rassid* and at the cafes, but I still couldn't find something to grasp onto in their world. Qassem galloped along the political trail while Assad seemed to me like someone sitting by the window, observing the movement on the street. He was a dreamer, a romantic who, were it not for his gentle manner and the love he had for others, could have stayed by the window his whole life, borne over the tumult, climbing the skies of poetry. But Assad didn't possess the right measure of selfishness needed by an artist; he accustomed himself to abrogating his own wishes to that of the community, that same tribal collective that confined him and led him to acts that he couldn't have been reconciled with. In this he wasn't much different from most Jews of his standing. As for myself, I hardly met with Jews and I stopped going to the Zawaraa club even before Jane left. I felt more and more that I had nothing in common with them. But I was always happy to meet Assad—he never failed to distinguish himself, it was just that I found myself at a crossroads then and I had to decide which way I was heading.

More than fifty years—is it possible to get all the details right after such a long time? The brain is already weary, knuckling under the weight of so many memories. Now I am trying to remember whether Assad's wedding was before Jane left or afterwards, and I simply can't reach a decision. I remember very well that I went to the wedding alone and regretted that Jane wasn't with me to see such a magnificent Jewish wedding. The guests filled the hall of the synagogue as well as the big courtyard adjacent to it, a military band played the wedding march to the jubilant sounds of the women ululating and the shower of candy raining down over our heads. The arrival of the military band was a surprise not only to the guests but to Assad himself who seemed quite moved by the official gesture accorded him. I remember describing every detail of the wedding to Jane, but I am simply unable to remember whether I did it in Baghdad or in New Orleans. Recast by the course of events, rent into the negatives of snapshots, you want to tell things in order and you can't.

What came first with Assad, the Jew or the Iraqi? It seems to me, were he asked such a question, that he would answer: Both are first. I believe him, because an answer like that unearths the dual nature of his personality, that same duality he bore with him his whole life only to be continually disappointed. A person can not be equally divided between two contradictory identities. And if that's what happened, doesn't it stand to reason that when it came to a test he would lose his ability to decide and find himself doing things his heart couldn't be at peace with? Wasn't it like that when he found himself pressured time and again to declare his loyalty to Iraq? What tipped the scales here, the Jew in him or the Iraqi? Neither. His duality tipped the scales, his lack of decision decided.

I loved Assad and I am making every effort to portray him in the fullness of his stature. No matter how strong my desire that what I write about him will once be read, there isn't a chance that will happen. These pages will remain buried in a drawer for a long time to come. I am trying to write the truth, and it's all the same to me whether I present myself in a good light here and there. It's not the reader's sympathy I'm asking for and besides, what good will such sympathy do me after I'm dead? There is one thing I want to say to Assad: Assad, my friend, despite everything, despite the resentment you harbored for me in your heart, my feelings for you haven't changed, and even now that you are settled in the state of the Jews, after the circumstances and not you decided your fate, I say to you in all sincerity that I still honor you!

Those years were a time of great change. The strengthening of circles sympathetic to Hitler and Mussolini worried me no less than it did Assad. But I was also repulsed by the failure of Jews to act. They lived according to some standard of validation whose time had passed—nor did they grasp the fact that there would be no more room for communal separatism in the new era Iraq was embarking on following the removal of Turkish rule. Iraq cried out for unity, even if tribal loyalties continued to inflame the instincts and incite bloody conflicts. In the urban centers at least, and particularly Baghdad, group loyalty took a back seat to society as a whole. The Jews were thoroughly urbanized and held key positions in all the governing institutions, over and above their dominance in commercial and economic life. But instead of bearing the burden in the national effort, taking their place in public life and political parties, they continued to revel in their isolation, fencing themselves in, under the perverse assumption that the good of the flock came first. This wasn't all—they even appeared impermeable to any patriotic feelings as they continued serving the British loyally, as lackeys and advisors. The Jews were the largest and strongest religious minority in Iraq, but what a difference there was between them and the Christians in Egypt and Syria who had been at the forefront of the movement for national renewal and independence. I was convinced then, and I still hold this same conviction, that the Jews misappropriated the historical role they had been given—but in this, the harm they brought was primarily upon themselves. Zionism celebrated its victories in Palestine with the support of the British, and the Jews of Iraq stood there aloof, some among them without even concealing their joy.

The empty declarations made by communal leaders and illustrious figures, all loyal Iraqis opposed to Zionism, did nothing to influence the instigators. Even the money they were forced to donate, supposedly for the struggle against Zionism, ended up in someone's pocket. This didn't help change anyone's opinion and just added to the general feeling that the only thing being paid was lip service, presented as a kind of tribute to the authorities, like a poll tax for protected subjects. They played the game they were expected to play in order to continue their separatist existence. People like Assad Nissim and a handful of other enlightened public figures added their hand to this game only to be used by those guarding the communal walls and power hungry politicians whose only desire was to guarantee their rule with the blessing of the British.

Assad was the most imposing figure in this tragic game, and when I think now about the celebrations that engulfed him shortly before his desertion, I feel sad for him, knowing that even through that artificial festivity he played right into the hands of the authorities. It was the unavoidable result of the duplicity of his character.

And what is he doing now in the Jewish state? Isn't he paying the price exacted from him, by still calling it "the land of promise?"

Assad was an exception amongst the leaders of the community, not just because he was a poet and edited a journal, but because he was a true patriot. In the mid 1930s, just before and right after Bakr Sidqi was overthrown, he often appeared at public gatherings in assembly halls or at mosques and even wrote some anti-British articles which caused him more than a little hardship. He was unique, a lone Jewish voice in the national campaign. I particularly remember a poem he wrote against the Italian invasion of Ethiopia, a poem that expressed the sincere sympathy of an Iraqi freedom lover for the struggle of an African people against fascist occupation. That was, it seems to me, after the article I wrote that left us at the brink of a real clash. I told him then that in that poem which had won such wide acclaim, his was the voice of every Iraqi patriot, and that I expected him to write against what was taking place in Palestine in the same spirit. He smiled without answering, and when I pressed him further, he said: "Against the Jews, I won't write a single word." I said against Zionism, and he answered: "Zionism I'm against, but don't forget that persecuted Jews are coming to Palestine, they are my brothers just as the Ethiopian people are my brothers."

Clear enough, with no need for interpretation. That's how Assad was. Dual loyalties. A soul split in two. He remained a loner, never joining any party, even though he was close to the circle around *al-Ahali* and he maintained friendly relations with Kamel al-Chadarchi, even appearing for the defense in the trial against him. As opposed to Qassem, for whom politics reached to the very marrow of his bones, Assad was the kind of person who didn't divide people according to their beliefs, just as long as they behaved respectably toward Jews. The interesting thing is that these two friends, so very different in their styles, never rebuked each other, as if they had an understanding between themselves. As for me, I had many collisions with Qassem, and I shall speak of them in good time.

A WHILE AFTER RETURNING from America, and before leaving for Cairo, I told Assad of the shameful spectacle I'd witnessed on the ship. Two Jewish families that boarded in Marseille announced their refusal to touch the food from the galley, and so the Captain proposed they cook their own meals and provided an area in the galley where they could prepare their kosher meat. But this act of good will on the Captain's side was followed by an absolute rejection of his request to permit a few Muslims from North Africa to also eat the kosher food. The Jews burst out in a rage against this handful of Muslims who were even willing to pay for the meals, and when I tried to tell them their Torah does not forbid them to offer their food to others, they yelled at me and chided me, calling me an eater of pork, tainted and unclean.

Assad heard me out with an amused smile, and mockingly said: "They probably saw you eat pork!"

I didn't reply. I was under a lot of stress at the time and did my best to avoid confrontations. But he caught me off guard when he began to talk about Reuben, that he was moving to Baghdad since the Hila power station franchise had been taken away from him. "It wouldn't be very nice for both of you to be living in the same city without being in touch." I asked him if he spoke for himself or for Reuben, and he said: "I'm an emissary." In that case, I said, tell him that, as far as I was concerned, he no longer exists, and it made no difference whether he lived in Baghdad or al-Hila.

I spoke with restraint, but Assad could see my anger, and quickly changed the subject.

An emissary. An eternal peace-maker. Reuben had turned Assad back empty handed in the past, and now he was enlisting Assad to carry through his intrigues. I should have told him this wasn't a respectable mission, but I didn't want to offend him. His motivation—to make peace—was pure. My anger was at how low Reuben was willing to stoop, sending Assad on this mission after other emissaries had failed.

I hated Reuben. Even now, fifty years later, when he already dwells in the dust, I can't even think of his name and not brim with venom. For me, he personifies everything contemptible in man and repulsive in the Jew. But sometimes I ask myself, had he behaved differently, had he not caused my separation from Jane, would I too have accepted the ambiguity, would I have found myself, like Assad, taking those loyalty oaths? The hand of god had saved me from such disgrace.

The last time I saw Reuben and my sisters was at my mother's funeral. News of her death was conveyed to me over the telephone, and as I listened a strange mood of sadness and exaltation overtook me. Her death cut me off from the family with finality and, if up to that point I had postponed crossing the thin line that separated me from Islam, with her departure I felt free of any obligation. My mother was very dear to me, and I felt her pain at being forbidden to see me and having to silently bear the shame that Reuben had brought on the family. Naima, on the secret visits she paid me, told of her suffering, shut up at home, refusing to see anyone. But after Jane left the tune began to change. Naima was already married and let herself take the initiative, once she even implored me to forgive Reuben to appease our mother. Jane had been the obstacle, and in her absence they imagined I could return to the bosom of the family! I told her that if he regrets what he did, it was Jane he had to ask forgiveness from, not me. She never mentioned it again but Reuben found ways to insinuate it to me, through other family members, until he even decided to mobilize Assad. Indeed, I should have told Assad that the role he took on wasn't at all honorable: emissary for an infamous zealot who had ruined my marriage and driven my mother to her grave.

This conversation with Assad was the last we had before I went to Cairo. I didn't reveal my intentions to him. Nor did I reveal the purpose of my trip at the office when I asked for a leave of three months. No one but Kazem knew the secret. I left early in the morning, accompanied by Sha'aban, to the Baghdad-Beirut station. I was calm, and at peace with myself. The tension was over, and I felt I was fulfilling a duty that was only natural for me to fulfill. I arrived in Cairo on August 25, 1936, and learned of a factor I could not have taken into consideration. I was told that according to Egyptian law, the Shari'a court can not confirm the entrance of a Jew or Christian into Islam without a written document from the religious institutions to which they belong stating that there are no objections. This law struck me as strange, especially since entering into the Islamic faith requires no special ceremonies and is carried out simply by saying the *shahada*. If the authorities wanted to follow Islam's high bequest, "No coercion in religion," I thought they had gone too far by giving rabbis and priests the privilege to do whatever they could to dissuade the candidate. I considered this an unjust nuisance and a violation of individual liberty but, on second thought, I realized how wrong I was. For Judaism requires a would be convert to undergo exhausting tests that often bring people to despair, and Christianity uses temptations and pressures, whereas

Islam not only refrains from either, it also asks for approval by the priests of both these religions! Is there better proof of Islam's superior morality?

November 7, 1936 is the date I became a Muslim by law, and since that day my name is Ahmad Haroun Saussan. I decided to keep my family name and my first name, leaving no room for slanderous accusations, that I was denying my origins. On the contrary, and I wrote about this in my book *My Path to Islam*, it was incumbent upon me as a Jew who had been shown the path to the true religion by God, to first and foremost address myself to Jews, entreating them to let go of their separatism and join the Muslim nation wherein they live.

My hosts in Cairo were members of the *Hidaya al-Islamiya* association. After Kazem wrote to tell them, they prepared for my arrival, held a party to honor me, and published an article in their periodical called "The Islamization of a Jewish scholar." During my three months in Cairo I stayed, for the most part, at the Nahdat Misr Hotel in the Azbakiyah neighborhood, and diligently worked on *My Path to Islam* and on getting it printed. The book came out with a forward by Sheikh Habib Allah al-Husseini of Najaf. The forward was a pleasant surprise to me, not at all what I expected when I sent Kazem some chapters of the manuscript to read. He approached the Sheikh, a figure he truly admired, and read him what I had written. The Sheikh told him: "Your friend is worthy of a warm welcome." He wrote that my path to Islam was inspired by the same spirit that moved the hearts of tribal Jewish chieftains to be counted among Muhammad's first messengers. He mentioned Ibn Ka'ab and Ibn Salam and Ka'ab al-Akhbar and others, those who were close to the Prophet and spread his teachings at the beginning of his mission. He also made sure to emphasize that had it not been for the intrigues of the Banu Sufian who fought the Prophet and incited the Jews against him, Banu Quraydha and Khaybar would not have turned against god's messenger. I was not convinced by this dubious argument, but was honored to have the name of such a celebrated Sheikh crown my book.

Kazem was among the very few in Iraq who knew my address, and in his letters he wrote how news of my conversion had reverberated. The story was highlighted in the newspapers and sparked an uproar among the Jews. In one letter he wrote that he met Assad; he wasn't surprised and said that, as far as he was concerned, this act wouldn't cast a shadow over our friendship. This was my hope too, but in reality things turned out differently.

DURING MY STAY IN Cairo, the Bakr Sidqi coup took place. Most of the chapters were already typeset and at the printer. All I had left to write was the last chapter, about Islam's affinity to Judaism and Christianity; I already had the basis of it with me, in its English version, the essay that I had submitted to Johns Hopkins University. The calm I was experiencing was disturbed by news of the coup and I was afraid I might have to go back to Baghdad before finishing the book and seeing it published. I called the Iraqi Consul, who was a friend, and he told me I had no cause for worry and, as soon as new directives arrived, he would let me know. And yet, I couldn't just remain stuck to my desk. I went out for a walk in the neighborhood. I was surprised by the public's indifference. Many people hadn't heard about the coup, and those who had didn't consider it important. To Egyptian eyes, Iraq was too far away to disrupt their daily routine. The press didn't give the event due coverage and simply delivered the story without any analysis. I stopped by the printer where I met one of the Hidaya al-Islamiyah activists—he was the only one that day to congratulate me warmly and lavish praise on the conspirators who had dealt Great Britain such a blow.

It took two days after the outbreak of the revolt for the press to shake off its skeptical caution and provide details on the turn of events. The signal for the revolt was given by three air-force planes that bombed the government palace by the banks of the Tigris, while an infantry regiment began marching from its base in Diala toward the capital. Minister of Defense Jaafar al-Askari was shot and killed by one of the commanders when he went out to meet the charging regiment; upon hearing this news, the Prime Minister and his band of cronies made a quick run for their lives. Among those who escaped were Nuri al-Sa'id and Rashid 'Ali al-Gaylani, a British henchman at the time. A new government headed by Hikmat Suleiman was formed and got the blessing of General Bakr Sidqi, leader of the revolt. I read every bit published about the revolt with great excitement and felt proud to have two venerated leaders in the government: Jaafar Abu al-Timman, and Kamel al-Chadarchi.

I called on the Consul's office every day to hear more details and to meet other Iraqis like myself, hungry for news. On one of these visits the Consul told me something that wasn't mentioned in the Egyptian press: one of the three pilots who bombed the government palace was Colonel Naji Ibrahim, the only Jewish pilot in the Air Force. "This should make you happy," he said with a smile. At the moment I was surprised but not so happy. But while I talked to the Consul and the others sitting with him, I thought that—if there were cause for joy—it wasn't simply for the lone incident in and of itself but for the proof it provided in favor of my argument canceling the Service Indemnity Bill, that this could provide a way to turn the Jews into an integral part of the national body. Naji

Ibrahim became a hero and his picture was all over the papers. How I longed to see Assad, to point out the mistake he had made. But the story ended up occupying me all of that day and it occurred to me that I ought to write an article conveying this news and my point of view to Egyptian readers. Yet, when I came to write it I couldn't stop at a short article without fully going into the entire phenomenon, and while I was at it I concluded that such a discussion belongs in the book and not in a newspaper article. The result was the conclusion I added to the book, one of the best chapters, I might add, if not the very best.

Were it not for this incident and learning of it when my mind was consumed by writing and final edits, I doubt that I would ever have achieved a concise formulation of my view regarding the question of reciprocal relations between majority and minority. The process of national formation in Europe that opened the gates for ethnic and religious minorities to join the main stream while maintaining their identity was my starting point in examining Arab society. Similarities between the changes that took place among Jews in Europe and the role played by Christians in the nationalist movements in Syria and Egypt are evident not only through participation in the struggle for independence and the immense contribution in the realm of culture, but also in the turn to radicalism in political philosophy and action. Minority-majority relations in Europe were like a pendulum swing between acceptance and rejection: as the majority tried to assimilate the minority, the minority struggled to protect its distinct identity—this was, in essence, no different from relations between Muslims and Christians from early in the last century. This pendulum hasn't yet, and probably never will, reach equilibrium. The simple reason for this is that the minority will never abandon its distinctive quality. That's how it was with Jews in Europe, and that's also how it was with Christians in the Arab world. Attempts by Jews in Europe to cling to the principle of secularism so as to remove an obstacle to acceptance were not merely ineffective, they also roused against them those fearing for the purity of the Christian nature of the state. This led to their total rejection, manifest those days in the expulsion of Jews from Germany. In view of this historical fact, I wrote, we must realize how hopeless the efforts of Christian radicals in the Arab world to deny religion its central role in shaping the nation are. In this, they do not merely serve as preachers for failed ideologies, they testify to their own disconnection and lack of comprehension regarding everything that has come to characterize Islamic society. Unlike Christianity, with its ancient feud against Judaism, Islam accepts and respects both Christianity and Judaism; it is therefore the duty of both Christians and Jews to repay measure for measure and shake off their separatism. Quoting the Egyptian Minister of Economy, Makram 'Ubayd, who said he was Christian by religion and Muslim by nation, I said that such words, lovely in themselves, can not salve the wound of duality that characterizes someone belonging to a minority; on the contrary, under special circumstances, such sentiments might even exacerbate the crisis.

I wrote the chapter in one sitting and when I was done I found it well structured and in need of no polishing or elaboration. I felt completely exalted, like someone facing a mirror and seeing, for the first time, that he is not deficient, that his body parts are well formed and in good shape, that his appearance is fine and normal like that of anyone else. No longer the outcast standing at the threshold, I am already inside, and my family is large and mighty and majestic!

Shimon Ballas

I DIDN'T EXPECT ENTHUSIASTIC congratulations from Jane after not responding to my first letter, but the harsh language she used when she replied felt like a slap in the face. I was sure that her father had dictated the words to her, and thought of turning to him directly in a letter of protest against his meddling in her life. But finally I gave up on this, lest she perceive my letter as ungratefulness on my part after all he had done and all he still intended to do for me. On my last visit I noticed that she was already growing accustomed to her new life, and the hints I threw out led me to think she wouldn't be happy to hear about my desire to convert. It was different in Beirut. She was willing to convert with me, though she wasn't required to, even if it was the only way out of the dilemma. I didn't have the courage then to share what I was going through and I chose the easiest way out that was offered to me. I never had much courage, for telling a lie takes courage too, and I couldn't lie and tell the family Jane had converted to Judaism before the wedding. Assad reproached me for telling the truth, but once done the deed could not be undone.

In retrospect I don't regret it, but here I would have to speak of things that can not be explained. Reason is an efficient tool for analyzing situations, sorting out problems, or making decisions, but it's a secondary tool; the primary tool is feeling, which reacts spontaneously all the time, every second. Feeling and reason contradict each other, and though they also appear attached, feeling obviously acts first, sometimes with utter disregard for reason. I say this because some situations in a man's life are hard to explain, and it is even harder, if not altogether impossible, for the very same person to account for them. On my last visit to America I became more convinced than ever that separating from Jane was unavoidable, that's why my conviction also grew that I saw no other way to make peace with my conscience except through the ultimate break with Judaism. Still, I knew that this act, suggested by losing hope of us ever coming together again, might deepen the breach, and yet it seemed to me that choosing this path could actually bring us closer again. I thought of the diplomatic post promised me as hitting two birds with one stone: going into the foreign service had been an aspiration of mine, but it also met Jane's needs in a roundabout way, removing the obstacles in our path.

When I got back to Baghdad I told Kazem that my mind was made up and I had no reason to procrastinate, but he tried to calm me down by saying: "For me, you are no less a Muslim than myself." He had tactical considerations, that my conversion might create a negative impression in light of the Foreign Office's willingness to assign me to a diplomatic post in London or Washington. He suggested I wait until the decision was made, and then no one would be able to claim I was forced to convert to win the appointment. In fact, I'd heard promises to take me into the foreign service since the first days of my return from America, after completing my studies. Whenever I inquired I was told unequivocally that my natural place was in the Foreign Office or in the Prime Minister's office, not in the City of Baghdad's engineering department, but beyond such talk nobody lifted a finger to keep their promise. Jane always complained about this, claiming I was treated like that because I was Jewish, and when I first visited her she told me: You are loyal to the homeland, but the homeland isn't loyal to you. She added: If you're going to be an engineer, don't waste your life demolishing houses and constructing roads! She may have been right, for had I taken her father's proposal and joined the architectural firm in Boston, surely I would have accomplished things I couldn't have even imagined in my limited function in the municipality. But such accomplishments weren't my first priority, and a professor's job in an American university didn't attract me, I aspired to other positions in which I could serve my country. I told Kazem: I don't care what people say, my path to Islam has nothing to do with trying to get ahead, but if my conversion makes it easier for someone in the government to make a decision, that's their business.

The Bakr Sidqi coup was a real shot in the arm for me. The Reform Government, as it was called, turned a new page in Iraq's political life and I was full of hope that it would succeed in carrying out the virtuous goals it had set. God chose to put things together, to mix my private life with the life of the nation; I too had turned a new page and everything that took place so far was over and done with. If there's any chance of Jane coming back to me, I told myself, it wouldn't be the result of writing a letter to her father or applying pressure; it could only come when she realized her mistake and understood my motives. But even if I remain nothing but Jimmy's father to her, as she wrote, she will always be the great love of my life. As for Jamil, only time will tell if he'll remember me. I felt reconciled, liberated from my guilty conscience, like someone reborn.

I stayed on in Cairo to see to the publication of *My Path to Islam*, and before going back I sent copies to the newspapers and various public figures. I took a hundred copies with me to give out, and asked for the rest to be shipped to me at home. Baghdad was at its finest hour then. People were excited, everyone talked passionately, some for and some against, and the press opened its pages to a new spectrum of public opinion. Baghdad went through a wave of freedom of expression in those days the likes of which it had never experienced before. And I was especially happy to see that Assad Nissim didn't just sit back and watch but turned *al-Rassid* into a political weekly. A few days after coming back from Cairo I read his

article "Why a Political Weekly," and decided to call and congratulate him. He sounded surprised, and his response was reserved at
first. I told him that I supported him and that I was proud of him,
my only wish was to assure him that our friendship would stand forever. He said that was his wish too, and jokingly added that he just
wasn't sure what he should call me now. The name you always called
me, I said, and he laughed: "Alright, I'll call you Abu-Hashem!" I
took this in good spirit, even though I felt his sting was off the mark.

OTHERS ALSO BEGAN ADDRESSING me by this name, but for the
municipal workers I remained "The Doctor", while Abu Jamil, the
name some friends used to call me, was gradually forgotten. During
my first days back at work I was inundated with visitors, and the
clerks did their best to greet them politely, although I could see confusion and impatience in their eyes. The Jewish clerks put me in
quarantine, eyeing me with animosity and whispering behind my
back. The Municipal Treasurer started sending his assistant to me
when he had a question, and every time I ran into him in the corridor that separated our two offices he'd look away. In meetings held
in his office or mine he'd talk to me without looking at me. Non of
this bothered me at all, I had immunized myself to acts of hostility
and knew in advance that life wasn't going to be easy, that conflicts
with the Jews were inevitable. The truth is that I didn't have any time
in those days to contemplate this. Political turmoil swept us in its
pulsing waves and every meeting with friends became a stage for
impassioned arguments. The freedom granted to political parties had
its effect on the public and controversies in the newspapers and open
gatherings sharpened the contrasts and even led to riots. Democracy
was making its first hesitant steps in the form of personal and ethnic

struggles and clashes. Jaafar Abu al-Timman's appointment to Minister of the Treasury enhanced the standing of the Shi'ites and there was much ado in government offices to give adequate representation to the Shi'ite majority. All this took place during an economic crisis. The state's coffers were empty, and it turned out that the ousted government had managed to dole out most of the money and the kingdom's property to its members and cronies.

My book didn't receive the response I had hoped for. Iraq was occupied by more important matters, and the papers were swamped with articles, reports, and manifestoes, and couldn't find space to discuss the book of a Jew who had converted to Islam. Apart from two or three reviews in *al-Yaqda*, and *al-'Alam al-'Arabi*, the other major papers, especially those with Jewish members on their editorial boards, ignored the book completely. In a random meeting with Assad I asked him if he read it. He nodded and said: "Don't expect me to publish anything about it." He didn't. A few months later he announced, to the surprise of many, the closing of *al-Rassid*.

Assad began keeping his distance from me, but Qassem couldn't hide his discontent: "I have not read, and have no time to read such a book," he responded to my question. He was entirely occupied by the political turmoil. His enthusiasm about the revolt didn't take long to cool down, and after al-Chadarchi resigned from the government he began speaking against Bakr Sidqi for overseeing the despicable massacre of the Assyrians in 1933, suggesting that he had been getting his orders through his German wife from ambassador Von Grobe! Similar attacks began to appear in the papers, and the leaders of the new regime were accused of leaning toward the Nazis. Supporters of Britain worked backstage and a sort of coalition was formed between them, liberal circles, and leftist groups, a coalition to take on the leadership of the revolt.

Kazem astounded me with his pessimistic forecast the very day I got to Baghdad. "Reform isn't carried out without means," he said, "the new government is weak and in discord, and the English lie in wait." He was right. The reform government lasted only about a year as a heavy curtain descended on the era of free speech and democratic life with a burst of gunfire at the Mosul airport that left the leader of the revolt wallowing in his own blood. The counter-coup put an end to a great dream in one fell swoop, and a new era of persecution and vendettas began. I found once more that my personal life was bound up and interwoven in the life of the nation, my dream to be appointed a diplomat expired too, submerged by the waves of upheaval that drowned the state.

If I were a historian I would choose the years 1935 to 1939 as a decisive time of transition from which to study the roots of the political transformations that followed. For some reason historians do not give these years the attention they deserve, providing the chronology of events without trying to examine their implications on the forties and fifties. The Bakr Sidqi revolt began an era of military coups not only in Iraq but in the entire Arab world; it was the tangible expression of the only option available to an opposition with no means at its disposal to mobilize public opinion, and ever since that time, each coup has called for a counter-coup. I recall a conversation with Qassem in the summer of 1959 in which I tried to find similarities between the coup of July 14th and that of 1936. He looked shocked. "How can you compare the revolt of a confused and tyrannical officer, who delivered the government into the hands of an even more confused Prime Minister, with a popular revolution such as this!" I told him that at the time the masses also supported the revolt, but he dismissed my words as groundless nonsense. The Communist party was in its prime then, its members came out of anonymity and obscurity in the prisons to assume key positions in the regime. Qassem himself leapt directly from the Nuqrat Salman prison in the desert to the Ministry of Information!

I will not pretend to have foreseen it all. I also considered the July 14th revolt to be unique in the history of Iraq, but what concerned me and led me to compare it with what happened twenty-three years earlier was the violent nature of strife between the parties, something that did not bode well for democracy. The Revolutionary Court's rumbling sessions set the tone for this, but Qassem had faith in the magic power of revolution, until its treacherous revenge branded his own flesh. Today he is a political exile in a country that lives under the Russian boot.

As I write this, the radio and television constantly broadcast news on the unfolding revolution in Iran. The Shah has surrendered and Khomeini is making his way back to his country from his recent place of exile in France. Sabry is optimistic. Among the leaders of the revolution is Bani Sadr, an acquaintance of his who studied in Paris and was Khomeini's right hand man. He believes Iraq would be first to acclaim the elimination of the Shah's regime. I try to take an optimistic view, like him, and hope the new situation will soon enable Zuhair's release. Only Butheina retains her doubts and refuses to trust the leaders of the revolution.

I telephoned the hospital. Kazem is still in the Intensive Care unit where he was moved two days ago, and no visitors are allowed. I pray for his recovery. How I wish he were with us.

EVENTS IN IRAN AND reactions in our country have disrupted my writing routine. A fortnight hasn't gone by since the outbreak of the revolution and already demonstrations against the Iraqi embassy have resumed, as well as allegations that Iraq persecuted Khomeini and was hostile to the revolution. Radio Teheran has launched a series of venomous tirades against Iraq as a collaborator with Israel and the United States, as wanting to reinstate the Shah and drown the Islamic revolution in torrents of blood. One can not believe one's ears. Such hatred after fourteen years of living among us? Jawad al-Alawi is not surprised. Khomeini's expulsion is not the cause of this hate, but the deeply rooted hatred of the Shi'ia. Indeed, that's how it is, this hostility never died down, but even so one can not ignore the progressive nature of a revolution that managed to overthrow a rotten monarchy and proclaim a republic. "That is the positive aspect," agrees Jawad.

At the Academy board meeting Jawad did not mince words in deriding the factional organizing of Shi'ite functionaries and the incitement of ethnic strife. We were all impressed. He is a principled man, a Shi'ite free of tribalism, just like Kazem. I said that such a clear voice warning against divisiveness ought to be heard throughout the country, not merely within the confines of the board room. I didn't mean anything in particular, but Moustafa al-Sharbati took my words as a proposal to make a public statement for unity, and before I could explain that I had no such intention most of those present expressed their support for the proposal. "We will declare our support of government policy," Moustafa said, "and warn the people not to listen to malicious elements who attempt to disrupt the unity of the people in support of the president." He even began drafting a text of the protocol.

"If we are agreed on the text we should make it public as soon as possible," said Mahmoud al-Janabi, sitting next to him.

"There is no text yet," Moustafa corrected him, "I'm only writing down the proposal."

"Read out what you wrote and we'll discuss it," al-Janabi replied.

I turned to Jawad to hear his response but he kept silent. Moustafa saw my look and smiled. "I have another suggestion," he said and laid his pen on the table, "Dr. Ahmad will compose the text."

"But you have already written," I said.

"You'll do a better job," he replied, with his annoying and fawning smile.

"There's no doubt about that," chuckled Shaker Khasbaq.

"A public statement falls within the Secretary's responsibilities," I tried to find a way out and turned to Jawad again.

"In my opinion we should consider if the timing is right," Jawad remarked.

"You have doubts about the timing?" Moustafa wondered, "You've said some harsh words yourself!"

"The question is whether it's the right time for a public statement warning about the people being divided," Jawad replied, "for by warning of such a danger we are close to admitting it exists."

"Leave such considerations to me," Moustafa quickly pulled rank. "The statement will not be made public without approval from the party and the President. If they think it better to wait, why then we've caused no harm, on the contrary—we've made it clear that we're concerned about the situation and can serve as an example for others."

Jawad didn't respond and the answer seemed to satisfy him, as well as everyone else present. But then all eyes turned back to me. "What do you think, Abu-Hashem? You are the most gifted of us all to compose a short and positive message," said al-Janabi.

"You see, we all plead with you," Moustafa placed a sheet of paper before me.

"You are the eldest member of the Academy, and the only one who stands above the ethnic dispute," al-Janabi went on merrily.

"We are all above the ethnic dispute," Jawad rebuked him.

"I had no intention, far from it," al-Janabi retreated.

I didn't respond. I'm already used to such insinuations. They see me as different. Not just al-Janabi, but Moustafa too, showing me his idiotic smile. And many others as well.

What actually perplexed me was lending a hand to an endeavor I wasn't fully in favor of. Taking a clear stance against irresponsible activists, as I had proposed, does not mean a show of solidarity with the government. I felt sorry that Jawad supported the public statement after he himself had more than once decried government policies against the Shi'ites in my very ears. Had he forgotten the blood bath two years ago, when the army attacked a procession of pilgrims coming out of Najaf with live ammunition? Has he forgotten the hundreds of detainees and those executed without trial, or tried in absentia because they're already six feet under? If one can not condemn the government, why must one praise it? And all the recent arrests, should these, too, be justified?

How in need I am of a wise word from Kazem! His condition deteriorates. He's been moved to the oncological department where, for the time being, he is undergoing an exhausting series of tests.

THE MEETING WITH THE President lasted only ten minutes, just the time it took the television crew to film us shaking his hand and standing next to him. On entering the office we saw him surrounded by a group of officers, browsing through maps that were laid out on his desk. He raised his eyes toward us, somewhat surprised, but got up immediately and the officers moved away to let us approach him and shake his extended hand. It was astonishing to witness the sudden change that came over his face once the flash-bulbs began snapping. He wore a big hearty smile and his gaze was acute and friendly, that of a healthy man aware of his own worth.

We waited over an hour in an adjoining guest room before we were called in. Upon arrival we learned that the delegation of the Writers Association had preceded us and already left the presiden-tial palace. Moustafa was furious and berated Maulud Takriti for admitting the writers in before us when the proposal to show our support for the President had been our doing. al-Takriti denied having anything to do with scheduling the visits and tried to be kind and praise our initiative. He sat with us most of the time but was occasionally called to the telephone or the office of the master of ceremonies. Other delegations began to arrive and he was asked to welcome them and decide whether to admit them to the President. He was a key figure in the party, a vigorous and resource-ful young man. I took him aside and asked if I could be allowed to have a few words with the President about Zuhair. He looked at me curiously: "What business is it of yours?" I told him Zuhair was like a son to us, and it was my duty to see to his well-being. "He's in good hands, you have nothing to worry about," he replied with a cunning smile.

His smile sent shivers down my back, but I insisted: "A word from the President would help."

"You think the President doesn't know who Zuhair is?" He asked in a threatening voice, "You think he doesn't know who his uncle is?"

"His uncle?" I was astonished. "What's that got to do with it?"

"I already told you that you better keep out of this," he replied and turned away from me.

I seated myself again, ashamed. Jawad put his hand on my thigh, as if to tell me to be patient. I was eager to tell him but Moustafa's presence, and his morbidly curious gaze, made me stop short. If the arrest was related to Qassem's activity, the story is much more complicated than we thought. Were his letters found among the papers and books they seized? Badriya said they'd emptied every drawer, slit open the mattress and pillow, searched every nook and cranny. Would they find it hard to produce incriminating evidence? But what is their goal? Maybe the whole story about connections to the Iranian underground is only a means to achieve something else? Will Zuhair have to pay now for what Qassem had done?

al-Takriti's menacing tone made me shiver. In their eyes, any means were permitted. Arresting the family members of someone on the run has become a legal procedure. Two years, at the very least, for each close family member, until the fugitive turns himself in. The wives are the first victims, and many of them were kept in detention for years, tortured and killed. And for Qassem, after remaining childless and always claiming he had no wife and sons they could persecute, for them to find Zuhair, his protégé, as a target of their schemes. I'm soaked in sweat, thinking of Badriya. What about her? Who could stop them? Who will raise their voice against these crimes? Amnesty International, whose reports are tossed into the garbage?

Sabry worries me. He acts without thinking, and everyone knows he is Zuhair's friend and comrade in the Maoist group—would it be hard for them to get their hands on him? How can I convince him to leave? Hamida doesn't understand a thing. All she can think of is the girl that would be left without a father. Butheina is the only one I can talk to but I won't tell her about this conversation. I won't tell a soul about this conversation. But maybe I'm wrong? What if al-Takriti didn't mean to threaten me, what if he adopted that tone just to keep me from bothering the President? You know who his uncle is? Who doesn't? Qassem isn't just some anonymous Communist, even though he is in Prague and Iraq is on friendly terms with the Czechs. Have him extradited? Forced back in by Zuhair's arrest?

I want to believe I'm mistaken. I wish my impressions were false. And how can I be sure Zuhair wasn't in touch with the Iranian underground? And what do I know about the nature of his connections with Qassem? Of the content of the letters they seized? But now their eyes are set on Sabry!

ACCORDING TO MY CALCULATIONS Badriya must be close to sixty. Looking at her sitting in Hamida's company, Qassem's voice reverberates through my mind: "I'm married to the revolution and the party is my family!" A flowery phrase he stuck to his whole life, but Badriya was real and her children were like his own. Most women her age were wrinkled and worn-out but she retained her beauty, her face smooth and delicate, the tattooed dot on her chin adding to her charm. She was about twenty-four when her husband died in a car crash and she hadn't been with a man since. Qassem was the man, and she stayed loyal to him just as he remained loyal to her.

I asked her if news of Zuhair's arrest had reached Qassem; she said he rarelycalled, but even if he did, she wouldn't be able to say anything to him on the phone. She was hoping for the best, and expected to hear something encouraging from me. What could I tell her? That Zuhair was being punished for Qassem's deeds? And what did Qassem do? Did he really operate a death squad? Those were the allegations of his former comrades, Communists who fought by his side and went through their share of torture and detention just like him. Hatred is cruel among the communists. The revenge of revolutionaries is cruel and horrifying. Anyone who steps out of line is condemned as a traitor, every disagreement deteriorates into a violent conflict, ending in assassination and bloodshed. But Qassem is not a violent man, I knew him to be honest and stubborn and I still believe in his integrity, even though I have no proof. His strong opposition to renewed collaboration with the Ba'ath was based on principle, while his friends rushed to renew their ties with those who had driven them from office and persecuted them. The rupture was inevitable and after it, a series of assassinations in the party began, blamed on him and his faction. Qassem fled and Aziz Laham became the primary informer, leading scores of his comrades to prison and death.

Qassem was a hardliner. I can find no better word to characterize him when I think of the extreme shifts in his positions since those far off days of the thirties. His objection to the Reform Government was justified by Hikmat Suleiman's support and admiration for Hitler, but after the German-Russian pact he changed his tune, saying we had to accept German help in our struggle against the British. He changed his mind again after Germany attacked Russia, and so on and so forth, from one extreme position to another, between prison and work in the underground, until the revolution got him out of Nuqrat al-Salman; from then on he'd had his ups and downs, detention and persecution and, finally, exile in his old age.

As I looked back on my relationship with him I came to realize that I never felt the same warm affection for him as I had for Assad. His severity kept me at bay. He had a ready answer for everything, delivered with the conviction of a judge. "Opportunist," is what he called me when I came back from Cairo. "A Jew doesn't convert to Islam because the light of truth has penetrated his heart. Don't tell me such tales!" And when I begged him to read the book first, he got aggressive: "If you want me to believe you, make a pilgrimage to Mecca, put on a kaftan and a Haj's cap and go to Najaf!" I told him he was being a demagogue and he laughed and grabbed my jacket: "Haroun," he shook me and said, "If you climb to the top of the minaret in the Souk al-Ghazl and yell out day and night that you became a Muslim for no other reason than love of Muhammad's nation, that wouldn't help you either!" Authoritative, aggressive, harsh with his words. That's how it was with Qassem. And yet, he wasn't malicious, always acting from an unflagging will to be right, to always have the last word.

He kept claiming that he hadn't read *My Path to Islam*. That was another one of his traits, to present an unyielding position that brooked no second thoughts. I didn't believe him, nor did I try to refute his attack. I knew then, and I know now more than ever, that he would tell me to my face what others said behind my back. He had heard rumors of the attempts to appoint me to a diplomatic post and, for him, that was evidence enough of my opportunism. As for myself, I was immune to such allegations. I desired the appointment, I wanted to be near Jane, but I had a ready answer for my offenders: Could anyone claim I didn't deserve the position? Could anyone claim it was given to me out of favor and not merit? But the proposal died under the power struggles between the Shi'ites and Sunnis, between followers of Germany and Britain, and I stayed on with the municipality. An engineer. Neither Consul nor Ambassador nor Minister nor Professor. Only the title stuck to my name. And who can even remember how I earned it? In retrospect, I should have taken comfort to be cleared of being an opportunist but, to tell the truth, I was deeply upset at not getting what I had asked for. In any case, Qassem stopped accusing me of opportunism but, every time we met, he made a point of speaking favorably about his Jewish comrades in the party, praising their loyalty and sacrifice. He wanted to tease me, and refute my claims about their separatism. I was also willing to admit that a major transformation had taken place among the young, at least until reality disproved us, and the entire community — with its elders and its children — uprooted themselves to Israel.

Qassem was wholly consumed by underground activity. For weeks he'd disappear from sight, but he always made sure someone was in his office to pick up the phone. Shortly before the war broke out he traveled to Europe; some say he went undercover to the Soviet Union to take part in an ideological seminary for senior cadres, but he himself never admitted it. I met him occasionally, but our friendship remained suspended until he was arrested in 1948, when it was renewed through Badriya. I had heard about his arrest at work and asked Hamida to visit her to see if she needed any help; since then she began calling on us several times a week, and Butheina made Zuhair her little make-believe brother.

Zuhair is thirty-three now, engaged to an Economics student; he looks a lot like Qassem, as if he actually was his son, and he studied law like Qassem, following in his path to political activism and detention.

As THE YEARS WENT by and separation from Jane became a fact, I grew used to living on my own, leaving the house early and coming back at night. Sha'aban prepared a light breakfast for me every morning, and I took my other meals out. The big house, remodeled to provide Jane and Jamil with the maximum of comfort, drove me away in its emptiness. I spent my evenings reading or writing an article for one paper or another. I created a new image for myself that wasn't much to be proud of, that of a commentator, quickly read and just as quickly forgotten. Being a civil servant I was kept from writing articles with political content; newspaper editors asked me to write memoirs about my years of study in America or give them translations and digests of articles from the English papers that I regularly got, anything that might pique their readers' interest. My tendency at first was to reject these offers—I wasn't a journalist, and I wasn't drawn to this kind of writing. But the empty hours of night and the urge to do something outside the work routine made me take up the pen and darken many pages without even a word of my own.

Reviewing articles and books was most in demand because in those days the Iraqi press drew its information solely from the wire services, mainly Reuters, and broadcast news. There were no foreign correspondents and editors needed up to date summaries on world events. There were few journalists with a command of English, and those who had it were, for the most part, Jews or Christians. Over time I found myself producing more and more commentary on political and social events in the world, commentary that lacked any personal dimension, objective writing so to speak, that quoted sources and took no stand. This was easy to do but never gratifying, although it won me many compliments. Readers were thirsty for anything that could open new horizons to them, bring them in closer touch with foreign worlds.

I am not very communicative to begin with and, under such circumstances, my natural tendency towards seclusion grew. My views were close to the moderate nationalist school of thought, represented by al-Chadarchi's party, but I refrained from any binding ties with the party, and tried to be as prudent as possible with the followers of Germany. The German Embassy was extremely active; it provided the press with ample material about German achievements in education and industry, held weekly screenings of films, lectures, and meetings with the Ambassador or guests he invited. I attended these events every now and then and tried to leave a good impression on every influential personality, no matter how crazy his views were. I had the uneasy feeling that, wherever I went, at the German Embassy or anywhere else, I must have been an object of infinite curiosity and suspicion. Jews did not come to the Embassy, and a good number of politicians and public figures stayed away from it. I recall one event that provoked numerous reactions in the press and almost brought about a diplomatic crisis. Ambassador Von Grobe imported a film about Hitler and all the Jewish-owned movie theaters refused to screen it. *Al-Yaqda* published a strong editorial and demanded that the government take steps against owners who prevent the ambassador of a friendly power from screening a movie. But the government chose to stay out of it, especially so as not to arouse the anger of the British Ambassador. Finally, the Ambassador was forced to show the film at the Embassy, to selected guests. I was invited, and watched a movie about a man who was a painter, loved children, and gave fiery speeches. On the way home I told Kazem that this man was scary. "That's what the Jews say," he answered curtly. I was annoyed to hear this from him, although I was sure it wasn't meant in irony.

I was so envious of Qassem, confident to the point where he didn't care about pleasing anyone. I reminded him once of the celebration of the Hindiyah dam, and the words that had left such a deep mark in my consciousness. He couldn't remember the conversation, and shrugged his shoulders. Indeed, he said what any boy like him might have said, anyone who aspired never to be enslaved into working the land. The son of a peasant, of one origin and one identity, not a hybrid like me. How I envied him!

The empty house weighed heavier upon me. Sha'aban was the only company I had, and he too suffered from loneliness. He would take long walks in the neighborhood and became stricter in his religious observance. He went to the mosque twice a day for prayers, prayed again at home, and every once in a while made a pilgrimage to the tombs of the saints. I observed this transformation with concern, and out of fondness and support began to join him for morning prayers. On the days of 'Ashura he'd join the processions of mourning and stay away from home all day. Once, I think it was in 1938, he came back all bruised, his chest bleeding. I was shocked at the sight and wanted to take him to a doctor but he stubbornly refused and retired to his room. After that incident I decided I had to do something to save him from this loneliness before it drove him insane. I proposed that he move his family in but he turned me down and said his wife wouldn't care to be away from her family, and that he had gotten used to visiting his own home once a month and on the holidays. Only after I used the imperative and told him his family would not be in my way, and and that it would actually please me, for I too was burdened by the house being deserted, only then did he go to the village and come back with his wife and four toddlers. They took the two rooms on the ground floor, and the house was filled with life and the smell of cooking. Since then he began to skip prayers during the day and only kept up with the dawn prayer. My days changed too, since his wife encouraged me to eat her cooking and I stopped having my dinner and, most of the time, my friday lunch out. The oven outside in the yard, which had stood cold for years, emitted the aroma of bread again now that Fatma baked daily. On Friday she'd bake an *'arug* stuffed with meat and onion and, on holidays, with help from the neighbors, she'd make *klayche* and other delectable pastries. The yard was alive all day: regular days were assigned for the washing, other days for sweeping the floors, beating the dust out of the carpets, heating the wash room. The change of seasons was marked by the days of squeezing tomatoes, to make a concentrate for winter, the days of date-honey preparation, drying okra and peppers on the roof, and storing provisions.

So the years went by, and the absence of Jamil and Jane became a desperate longing, a faraway dream shrouded in another era. Jane would send me Jamil's photographs, especially from his birthday parties, with which I decorated the wall next to my desk. Fatma admired every new photo she saw of Jamil. She didn't care for Jane, and never asked about her but, one day, after placing a tray on the dining table, she remained standing and looked at me. "Don't laugh at me," she said apologetically, "but you are dearer to me than a brother—take this and send it to her." She handed me a small bundle, about the size of a nut, and asked me to send it to my wife to hide in the folds of her dress. That would cleanse her heart of the Devil's delusions and with the help of god, she'd come back to me. I thanked her and promised to do as she said. I did not want to disappoint her.

In April, 1939, Iraq was in turmoil again. King Ghazi lost his life in a car accident. The car he was driving crashed into a power line pole and by the time the bloodied body was pulled out of the wreck his spirit had departed. It was the tragic end of a licentious king whose debauchery was the talk of the town. Unlike his father, known for his integrity and Spartan habits, Ghazi was a womanizer, drank a lot, and was addicted to horse races and wild driving. So death found him, intoxicated, racing his car. And yet there were rumors that the accident was staged, that he was murdered by his opponents and then put in a car that was crashed into the power line pole. These rumors were later confirmed by people close to the court who said the murder was coordinated with the British, happy to get rid of him for his support of the pro-Germans. His death was a blow to the pro-Germans, and government policy aligned itself with British dictates. Heavy clouds were gathering over Europe at the time, the Second World War was at the gate, and in September of that year Hitler attacked Poland.

The days of mourning for Ghazi were a time of mass processions on al-Rashid Street. On the day of the funeral many delegations arrived from all parts of the kingdom to pay respect to the late king. The offices of the municipality became a gathering place from where delegations of mourners left for the palace. I also marched with municipal workers, among the flag bearers and wailers in a procession resembling those of the 'Ashura. I remember the wailing chanted by thousands of mouths to the beat of blows on exposed chests: "Ghazi is dead and the enemies rejoice, God save Faisal the Second!" The procession stopped for a while near the bridge, and I withdrew to the sidewalk and observed the rest from there. I saw Assad marching in the first line of the Jewish community representatives. His face was sealed, and he looked as if he just happened to find himself amidst the frenzy. We rarely met in those days, but the break had not yet taken place.

THE CHANGE THAT CAME over the house since the arrival of the Sha'aban family interrupted the somber routine that had once dominated it, but with time this change too became routine. I grew accustomed to the everyday commotion in the big courtyard, to the noise made by the children, to the festive nature of Fridays, to the appearance of women from the neighborhood who came to help Fatma and keep her company. This family's world became part of my world even though I wasn't directly involved in it and, in spite of all my attempts to cross them, boundaries were carefully maintained. For family members and Fatma's friends I was the "Bey," and the women would cover their faces and silence the children whenever I walked in. Do not disturb the "Bey," the "Bey" will get angry, god save our "Bey"—whispers to that effect would steal into my ears as I went up the stairs to the second floor. The children were not allowed on this floor, and its three rooms stood empty the year round. The study, in the new wing, was the only place I spent my free time; the bookshelves were there, the large drawing board, the writing desk, two chairs and a couch. I only saw people in the living room on rare occasions, and weeks would go by without anyone entering it except Fatma when she came in to clean.

I adapted to this routine and was determined to go on living like this and not share my days with a second wife. Concealed somewhere in my heart was a desperate yearning, doomed to remain unfulfilled. During the long nights, seated in a chair with a book in my hand, my mind sometimes wandered and got lost in the entrails of a bottomless maze. I reflected on the condition of a man marked by a sense of foreignness, unable to root it out. Such a man resembles one who adapts his clothing to circumstances so as not to look different or out of the ordinary, but can not adapt his behavior to the clothes. Worst of all, even if he manages to behave according to circumstances, this would appear strange to those around him and emphasize his foreignness even more. A man's image depends on the perception of those around him and that, in turn, depends on the things deeply ingrained in him. Acceptance? Nothing motivates man as much as the desire to be accepted, not just as one of many but as someone unique and special. Sha'aban's family was part of my world, but I was kept outside its world. I liked to squat on the floor and eat with them, the way I did as a child, avoiding my father and brother's watchful eye to join my friends the peasant children. And I did sit with them a few times, but this seemed so unnatural to them that my presence took away the joy of eating, and instead of removing barriers I found myself making them uncomfortable and endlessly puzzled. It saddened me as I again realized that I had to accept my predicament and carry my foreignness wherever I turned, accept not being accepted just the way I had been in the past, a Jew from without, as Assad had put it, and now I was a Muslim come from without. Every now and then I found some comfort when I told myself that Jane also had to be experiencing a sense of foreignness in the natural surroundings she had returned to since she carried—in her soul and the eyes of those around her—the indelible mark of one who had crossed borders and donned the garb of others.

My mind sometimes wanders to those distant years of childhood in al-Hila, to the house I grew up in, always alive with the sound of work carried out on regular days: slaughtering chickens and preparaing *hamin* on Friday, slaughtering a lamb for Rosh Hashana, building a *sukka* in the yard and decorating it, the week of baking *matzoth* for Passover. Purim gave me an opportunity to show my readiness to fight by putting on a lion's mask or being a wild Indian shooting my pistols in every direction. How great was my joy to have my new clothes, tailored for the holidays, the spotless white suit I would wear for Rosh Hashana and Yom Kippur, when my brother and I accompanied my father to synagogue. I was especially proud of the new shoes, they hurt my toes alright, but they also made a sharp squeak that paced my tread like a marching tune. I recall that even then my joy was mixed with unease at the sight of the peasant children in worn-out weekday clothes, eyeing me enviously. I wasn't allowed to visit them in my new suit; it wasn't only my celebrated Judaism that kept me apart from them but my loftier status too. Only later, as an adult, did I realize how great the injustice was, that we Jewish children had our holidays for our exclusive joy, while Muslim holidays were like holidays for us too. We celebrated 'Id al-Fitr and 'Id al-Adha with them, and on the night of Mihya, in the middle of the month of Sha'aban, we used to play with Muslim kids, setting up bonfires, lighting sparklers and flares and other fireworks. The sense of injustice that pierced my soul at the time later forced me to consider the inconsolable contradictions of minority/majority relations. For in the ongoing struggle between the force of assimilation on the one hand, and the force of protection on the other, the preference given to the minority over the majority stands out in its strangeness, as the minority maintains its distinction while it is taken to be part of the general public. The holidays were but one aspect of this preference, and made me compose the article demanding discontinuation of that unacceptable custom of recognizing the right of Christians and Jews to miss work on their holidays.

In those days my heart was heavy when I thought of Jane. Even now, as I recall that memory and put it in writing I'm caught in a dismal state of mind. I wasn't saddened by the boycott my brother imposed on me and by being ostracized by the community as much as I was to see Jane in her loneliness. There were no holidays in our home; except for birthdays and the New Year's ball at the

British Ambassador's residence, we had no days of celebration like everyone else. Even the food the Armenian cook made for us smelled and tasted different from anything else cooked in the neighborhood. The house was like an island and no neighbor ever came in, though they kept a suspicious and curious eye to whatever went on in it, gesticulating amongst themselves: "The American woman's house." Now, I would tell myself in a kind of stoic acceptance, the neighbors point to the house with the polished brass sign affixed to the door as the "Bey's House," and whisper: A Jew who became a Muslim and his wife deserted him.

WHEN I HEAR NAZEM al-Ghazali singing "The Mousayav Bridge," I hear echoes of Umm Farhan's pure voice. A stocky woman dressed in black, she lived in a hovel near the Jewish neighborhood. She used to sit in the courtyard of the ruins, strewn with rocks and pigeon-droppings, and light a fire beneath a charred pot. Her face was round, tattooed, her big eyes accentuated by thick black kohl. I never saw her outside her house, which was nothing more than a tall mound of rocks, with an opening covered by a piece of faded fabric. Behind that fabric a tiny room survived, the remainder of the collapsed dwelling, in which she lived with her son Farhan or, as everyone called him, the Pigeon-Flyer. A flock of pigeons of all colors inhabited the hovel with them and Farhan used to climb to the top of the mound to fly them with a long stick. The stick was a palm branch with the leaves plucked off and a rag tied to one end. The flock would fly over the hovel and respond to Farhan's stick. It would fly all the way to the fields on the other side of the river, turn to the little gate at the end of town, then glide over the neighborhoods of Hithaween, Ta'is, Mahdiya and Jibareen, and every time it approached the hovel Farhan would gesture with his stick and the flock would continue flying through the blue, the setting sun illuminating their flapping wings in a spectacular gleam. Each day, at a set time, just before the muezzin's call for evening prayers, Farhan would mount the mound as the pigeons responded to the clicks of his tongue and soared off in a great clamor. Their flight went on only as long as Farhan stood atop the ruin; once he threw his stick down, the pigeons knew it was a sign to end their run and they would land all at once in the yard where Umm Farhan fed them seeds.

The ruin had an aura of mystery. Umm Farhan and her son were not natives of al-Hila and I don't remember ever being told where they came from or when they settled in that hovel. They were alien in their surroundings, secluded in their own world, and the life of the town passed them by without touching them. Neighbors never visited and, in the Jewish neighborhood, the mothers used Umm Farhan to scare their children. "Umm Farhan will kidnap you if you don't. . ." My mother didn't threaten me with Umm Farhan, but she always warned me never to go in to their place; like all the other kids, I was drawn there to look at the beautiful pigeons. She's a dangerous woman, they told us, who talks to ghosts and demons. Farhan wasn't popular either, and mentioning his nick name was enough to make heads nod and faces grimace. Someone who tended pigeons was considered a deviant; in those days, it was almost like being a brigand or a pimp. And yet, no one harmed them, and everyone always marveled at Farhan's pigeons. Some folks would stop work when they saw the colorful flock fluttering overhead and get ready for prayers even before hearing the call of the muezzin; everyone knew Farhan performed his daily ritual with astounding punctuality. Wearing a white *dishdasha* with black stripes that reached down to almost cover his bare feet and wrapped in a thick camel-hide belt, Farhan would stand at the top of the mound and utter guttural exclamations that only the pigeons understood. He produced other sounds too: whistles and snorts and slurps and a choking noise, while the pigeons answered with all sorts of gurgles and hums, flapping their wings, landing on his shoulders, and putting their beaks in his mouth. Like King Solomon, Farhan could talk to the pigeons, and this remained a wonder to the kids who felt drawn to him as if he were bewitched.

But it wasn't only the pigeons that drew us to Farhan, it was the kites he built in a rickety shed behind the mound of rocks, not visible from the entrance to the hovel. There we found him immersed in his craft, looking serious, and he ignored our presence. He never reproached us or ran us out, but we were awestruck by his silence and watched him mutely, afraid to interrupt the magical silence. He built two kinds of kites, small light ones that he sold us for two bits, and big decorated kites that he refused to sell and wouldn't even let us touch. The big ones, known as *Umm al-Sinatir*, were made of thick paper, usually conical, with variegated pipes and paper chains, and a long tail that branched out into ribbons and had minuscule bells attached to it. He'd fly these kites himself, when he went up to the top of the mound, and they'd soar to the heart of the skies, spreading their wings like doves and waving to the entire town from their majestic heights. At times he tied the string to a wooden post, and the kite would remain stable, unleashing its delectable tinkling into the quiet night.

The pigeons' breathtaking flight, the kites' distant chime, and Umm Farhan's pure voice singing "The Mousayav Bridge" adorn my most beautiful memories of the city of my birth with a dim and pleasing pain:

The town sleeps quietly and
My eye knows not slumber so
I ask a star in the night so deep,
Oh why, oh why won't
my love come back ,
Rescue me, oh merciful folk,
From the menacing scorners
Who left me alone
on the Mousayav Bridge

A song that grew in the fertile valley of the Euphrates, by the banks of the river and in the palm groves, in the wheat fields and Bedouin tent encampments, a song of sorrow that infuses the heart with infinite yearning. The Great War carried Farhan away in its storm. The Turkish governor laid a heavy hand on the populace, his troops raided homes, handcuffed the men and dragged them into long lines, like cattle to the draft. Farhan disappeared. Some said he escaped and was never caught, others said he was drafted and died in the war. The uprising against the Turks spread all along the middle Euphrates, and in spite of the cruel oppression and public hangings, the flame of rebellion did not die out until the Turks left. Those were days of fear, and Umm Farhan was left all alone in the ruins, her voice no longer pure and piercing to the quick but rent by sighs and soaked in tears, the voice of a desperate elegy. *Umm al-Sinatir* no longer flew in the sky, and her chime no longer carried a lullaby to those sleeping on the rooftops. The pigeons no longer flew in their festive circles and the men no longer matched their prayer time with Farhan's climb to the top of the mound. We moved to another house, outside the Jewish neighborhood, and shortly after that I myself moved to Baghdad to continue my schooling. On one of my visits I found the ruin all empty, with only cats slinking among the rubble. No one could tell me what had become of Umm Farhan.

The wheel of destiny never tires of turning. In the mean time, a second World War broke out, and many peoples were washed away by its rumbling waves. I remember that in 1944 I visited one of the local cafes on the Karkh bank of the river, to meet the poet Mula 'Abud al Karkhi, near the *Karkh* newspaper building. Mula 'Abud owned the paper and was the editor in chief. *Al-Karkh* played an important role in the struggle against British rule in the twenties and thirties, thanks to the editor's poems, in colloquial Arabic, that covered the front page. His tongue was sharp, and no word, no matter how crude, was too low for him to attack someone who aroused his rage. Many maintained an air of caution toward him, trying to ingratiate themselves by giving him all kinds of gifts just to avoid his poisonous arrows. When I met him, he'd already closed *al-Karkh*, due to old age and ailing health, but he kept publishing poems in other newspapers. And it was in one those that he happened to come out with a poem of mockery against the Mayor, full of obvious hints and insinuations of corruption. The Mayor's cronies advised him not to sue the man, but to try and shut him up by other means. And since the poet's ire was the result of a construction permit denied to one of his relatives, I was asked, as the chief engineer, to negotiate with him and propose some minor changes in the building plan so it could be approved. I didn't embark upon this mission willingly, but to my surprise I found a pleasant conversationalist who liked to tell jokes. The disagreement was settled easily and, the following week, al-Karkhi published a eulogy for the Mayor, arguing that one of his noblest traits was his sense of humor!

I only came to tell of al-Karkhi and his mischief in order to finish the portrait of Farhan that I began. I was distracted from my conversation with the poet when I heard the proprietor of the café call one of the waiters Farhan. I looked at the tall thin man, dressed in a striped *dishdasha* and a camel-hide belt. He and no other, as if he'd stepped out of the underworld and begun walking among the cafe guests in his bare feet, a serious look on his now meager and wrinkled face. I called to him, and asked if he was Farhan the pigeon-flyer and kite-maker, and he stared at me indifferently without replying. And when I went on to remind him of his days of glory, a dim spark came to his eyes, and he muttered: "Let me be, god have mercy on your father."

That was my last meeting with Farhan. A lonely introvert washed off his command post atop the mound by the ebb and tide to spend the rest of his days in a noisy, filthy cafe. What remains? The memories remain: The marvelous flight of the pigeons, the chime of *Umm al-Sinatir*, and Umm Farhan's elegy still making the heart strings tremble.

THAT YEAR, 1944, MY life took a turn. I got married in April, and left the municipality in September, when I was appointed head of the National Lands Administration. That year I also forsook my childhood name, and since then the name Haroun did not appear on any document that bore my signature. Ahmad Saussan was my full name in government ministries and in public, and except for Qassem, no one addressed me as Haroun any more. In fact, I had decided to drop this name when I ordered a new sign for the house in Karada, where I was forced to move. Hamida didn't like the house in Bab al-Shaykh; more than anything, though, she couldn't stand the presence of Sha'aban and his family. She demanded that I send them away and put me in a difficult position that touched my very conscience since I was the cause they had uprooted themselves from their native village and, after years of dedicated service, after they'd grown accustomed to life in the city, my heart forbade me to send them off to fend for themselves. But Hamida insisted, and her father showed no willingness to talk to her; for him there were no obligations to servants—in one home today, in another tomorrow, and there was no reason to get worked up over servants. He was an old guard feudalist, and servants were like slaves in his eyes.

The question had come up even when we were engaged, and I could foresee harsh days ahead. I begrudged Kazem for incessantly pressing me to change my way of life and establish a Muslim family as required by religion. His initiative to approach the father and serve as my matchmaker particularly irked me. If this is how it starts, I told him, I hereby annul the engagement, I am happy the way I am, and have no need for a wife and kids. But Kazem wasn't one to give up easily, and he kept prevailing upon me until he proposed a solution I could accept, moving to a new house and looking for ways to compensate Sha'aban.

I saw something symbolic in this solution, because a new life deserved a new environment. The house in Bab al-Shaykh— memorial shrine to my loneliness, where every nook and cranny spoke to me with orphaned echoes from the most beautiful time of my life—might have kept me chained to the past and put obstacles between me and my young wife. It was a wise and practical solution, but in order to realize it I was forced to delay the marriage by some months till I could find an appropriate house and prepare it for comfortable living. It took me that long to set up Sha'aban with a job as a janitor in the municipality, rent a three-room house for him in a nearby side street, and pay two years in advance as some sort of compensation.

Hamida wanted to move to one of the new neighborhoods, beyond the eastern gate, where the city found itself expanding over a wide agricultural district: houses adorned with gardens, known at the time as European, wide streets and boulevards that the municipality, and I myself as Chief Engineer, worked hard to make beautiful and keep green, as opposed to the old city, cramped with its narrow alleys. These neighborhoods were magnificent but typical for the Baghdad of those days, Jews were the first to occupy the new houses; even as construction was just beginning, the area was populated by Jews and a smattering of Christians. The neighborhoods of Tawrat, where the ancient synagogues were concentrated, Taht al-Takiya and 'Aqulyia, and the all the rest of the Jewish neighborhoods, delivered hundreds of families, joined by other families from nearby cities. Baghdad attracted the Jews and the years of the World War were a time of prosperity for them, a time to accumulate assets. Their domination of essential branches of the economy went beyond any proportionality to their numbers. Banks, international trade, insurance companies, automobile and electronics imports, the railway administration, movie theaters, the horse races — each single sector that was initiated or had expanded since the British came in during the First World War was effectively directed by Jews. In my work for the municipality I ran into them at every turn, be it as proprietors and brokers, or in the faces of one clerk or another that had taken a position in government ministries. In my affairs with them I had to avoid any breach of the formal, and they too kept a distance, so the business before us was settled quickly. And yet, some of them were rude, trying to provoke me by addressing me in the Jewish dialect, especially when others were present. Those petitioning the municipality annoyed me the most. I made it a point that no Jewish petitioner be directed to me, and in spite of this they'd sometimes sneak into my office and address me with despicable flattery: You're no stranger, you're one of us, you understand us! When I was Jewish they regarded me as a stranger, not one of them, but to get what they wanted they were willing to adopt me!

I wanted to keep as far away from the heavy concentrations of Jews as possible. To do that, I had to go as far as the Karada quarter—there I found a house surrounded by a large garden that pleased Hamida after she paid it a visit with her parents. Indeed, this was a year of change in my life. A new house, a young wife, and a way of life I was unused to. Hamida was twenty when she married me, but as opposed to what might be expected from a young woman who grew up in a conservative home in the Muntafaq district and whose entire education consisted of four years of primary school, she had a passion for all the latest styles she'd been exposed to in Baghdad's wealthier homes. Garden parties on the lawn, ballroom dancing, large dinners on the holidays and for various occasions, and a weekly day for receiving visitors, *kubul* day. All these events required the appropriate attire, and she had the chauffeur at her disposal for her shopping sprees and visits to the seamstresses who were, for the most part, Jewish. I was thrust from my quiet routine in Bab al-Shaykh into a daily tumult in which I couldn't find a minute of peace for myself. When I snuck off to my room to rest my mind, Hamida would send the maid to call for me or come by herself to reproach me: "With your books again!" With no other options at hand I began staying late at the office, after everyone else had left, justifying my late arrivals home by talking of my new position at work and the responsibilities that came with it.

I was supposed to be happy, and I drew quite a bit of pleasure from the commotion around the house; of course, the presence of a young woman nourished my manly ego—what more could a man ask for, as the saying goes—than respect, income, and a loving wife? But I knew no real happiness, and even after Butheina was born, which made me very happy, I'd get caught up in doleful reveries and an intense desire would burn in me to see Jane and Jamil, my firstborn son.

"I'm glad you worked it out for yourself."

"I followed the conventional path."

"It's better this way."

"I always aspired to go my own way."

"You've done that too."

"I made a mistake, we both did."

She didn't reply. Later she said: "I felt sorry you were alone for so many years. Every letter you sent troubled my conscience. But now I'm happy for you."

"This is something I can not say to you."

"I've gotten used to that," she sighed. "Jimmy fills my life."

She didn't say much about Larry. His picture stood on a chest of drawers. A handsome man, a pilot smiling in an officer's uniform. I thought of my own picture in an officer's uniform, the one that took Jane by surprise. What a twist of fate!

"The world has changed," I said.

"Yes," she replied, animated again.

"The Zionists won."

"Does that make you angry?"

"It depresses me."

"I understand. But the Jews deserve a state, after all they have suffered."

"Not at the expense of another people."

She nodded in agreement, and I didn't raise the issue again during the visit.

I did talk with Jamil though. He was sixteen, and like many his age in those days in America his sympathies for the Jews were almost predetermined. "Mother thinks like me, and so does Grandpa," he'd tell me every time I talked of the injustice done to the Palestinians. With Zionist propaganda, and the shame of the Arab defeat, could one have expected anything else? All this made me sad, although I found Jamil to be a clever boy, even-tempered, and full of good will. He was a consolation, and I told Jane as much. "He is like you in everything," she replied with a soft, attentive smile.

No, Jane, he's like you, he has your pure heart!

I DIDN'T HAVE A REAL conversation with Assad Nissim until September, 1939; if we ran into each other, we'd just exchange greetings and go on our way. I remember that the only conversation we had of any substance was on the phone, after he closed *al-Rassid*. I called him and he told me about the difficulties he'd been having with the man in charge of publications; he served as a censor and demanded to see every article and poem, arbitrarily ruling out what seemed to him beyond the periodical's permit. "Times have changed," he said sadly, "and any ignorant dimwit becomes a man of power, there's no one to talk to." I told him that closing the magazine would leave a gap in the free press, and he said this gap was being filled by Von Grobe's agents. He added: "I've carried out my duty for seven years, and now it's time to take care of my family and pay the debts I've accumulated." We spoke as friends, but nothing more. Neither he nor I suggested meeting.

A year later the war broke out. In September I met him at a big gathering of high-school graduates summoned to the Military College in Karada East, about to be drafted for reserve-officers training. I recognized many acquaintances there, including quite a number of Jews. And I met Qassem, who looked nervous and worried. "I don't like this game," he said. "Who do they want us to fight? Against Hitler with Britain, or against Britain with Hitler?" I told him: "We'll fight for Iraq," and he blew air through his lips in response. That's about all he could do to express the growing feeling among the public and the alienation of the educated, when the political leadership leaned toward Germany, while the government stood by Britain. I tried to come back at his derision by asking: "Doesn't the revolution need trained officers?" This time he replied seriously: "The masses make the revolution, not officers."

While we were talking Assad joined us. "And so we meet," he said with his amicable smile.

"We'll asked to be assigned to one unit," I said.

"Don't rely on me," Qassem objected.

"If this is a game, we'll play it together," I said.

"I won't be ordered to play," he insisted.

Assad and I exchanged smiles. We both understood why he resented the draft. Russia had taken a neutral stand on the war, and a revolutionary like him would not participate in a war between imperialists. But this wasn't the time for a political argument, even more so since some other friends had joined us and several conversations began going at once.

Due to the disorder, and the small number of registration clerks, we were kept waiting on the inner college square well into the evening. The next day we were supposed to report for duty with our bundles and get sent to training units, but about half the draftees didn't show up again. Qassem didn't show up either, and I have no idea under what pretext he was released or who used their influence to intervene in his favor. Be that as it may, those released knew how to use the various available means to dodge nine months of service. I found myself in a very awkward situation. The Mayor objected to my being drafted, and in spite of my vigorous protests he obtained a release for me, claiming that my work for the municipality was vital, and that I had already gotten my military training as a student in America. I decided to show up anyway, and talk to the recruiting officer, hoping that I could persuade him this release was obtained against my will. The officer looked at me the way you look at a madman. People moved heaven and earth to be released, and here was a man in a prominent position who demanded to be drafted! "I can't help you, the order came from higher-up," he told me, his smile mixing irony and apology.

As I left his office embarrassed and confused, the first person I saw was Assad. "I've got a problem with the Mayor," I told him before he could ask, and told him what the Mayor had done against my will.

"I understand him," he replied.

"I'm sad," I said. "Believe me."

"And where are all the great patriots?" He looked around.

"And you?"

"I'm fulfilling my duty."

"I asked about his work," and he told me he had closed his office because he didn't have a partner; as for his work as legal advisor to the Rafidayin textile company, it had been put on hold until his release.

"I could have gotten out," he said, "but I don't like to shirk my duties."

"There aren't many like you," I said truthfully.

We went on talking for a little while, and when I reiterated my sadness at being blocked from the draft he replied with some scorn: "Take comfort in the fact that quite a few Jews have stayed and will be officers in the army."

"If that's a comfort, you must have changed your mind," I replied.

"And what was my position before?" He asked.

"But that's exactly what we disagreed on! Now the Jewish youth will also get pre-military training," I said, referring to legislation enacted that year, requiring all students in the country to join the Futuwa corps.

"The disagreement stands," he replied. "They also made the Jewish youth wear uniforms in Germany, and what came of that?"

"Isn't that a little harsh," I protested.

"I wish I was wrong," he retreated, as if trying to end the conversation.

That's how he always was. He spoke his mind but avoided confrontation, leaving things to hang without an adequate explanation. His apparently calm and even temper inoculated him against attacks, not giving his opponents the opportunity to get angry at him. He knew how to give the impression that he wasn't angry at anyone either, and if his interlocutor disagreed he would mention what he thought in passing, as if it were just a fleeting notion. But all this was on the surface because, deep down, he really was a sensitive man and only those who knew him well could appreciate his restraint.

I went back to my routine. There was a lot of work at the municipality. Paving the road named after King Ghazi required the demolition of old congested neighborhoods, some of them inhabited by

Jews, and the municipality was faced with complex and arduous tasks: to render land ready for construction in the south, and do battle in the bidding war for land along the new road, with speculation getting more and more outrageous as the paving advanced. At night I would come home and shut myself up in my room. I stopped writing for the press and embarked upon an ambitious plan, to compile a historical map of Baghdad. After twenty years of intense work, my plan yielded the *Historical Atlas of Baghdad*. I studied numerous maps charted by geographers and orientalists such as Herzfeld, LeStrange, Strick, and others who relied on ancient maps and the itineraries of Arab and foreign travelers. While I was doing this, I became immersed in careful readings of Ibn Hawqal, Ya'aqubi, Ibn Jubayr, Ibn Juzi, Yaqut Hamwi, Ibn Khalikan, and dozens of other historians and geographers. Beside the rich information about the city's topography, its climate, and the floods of the Tigris, this reading gave me great satisfaction in my long hours of solitude. The war in Europe occupied me no less than it did others, but in the evening and during the night I tried to cut myself off from the cares of the day and work on piles of preparatory drafts for charting the round face of Mansour City. Hitler's armies occupied Europe in a flash, humiliating France, and began threatening the British Isles. Hitler's victories filled the public with complacent optimism, and many anticipated Britain's surrender and the capitulation of the great Empire over whom the sun never set.

It was hard for a man like myself, educated in the West, to share this optimism, and yet I rejoiced at the British downfall, to see them facing a stronger enemy who could trample their pride. This ambiguity was shared by leftist circles and al-Chadarchi's party; they couldn't, with all the contempt they had for Nazi ideology, sympathize with the power that ruled Iraq by force. But I was embarrassed—and I have no reason to deny it—by the pro-German propaganda. After ignoring my book, *My Path to Islam*, for three years, someone happened to remember it and since then the book had become a handy source for all kinds of quotations, used to prove the validity of race theory and taken as the testimony of a Jew about the Jews! I was deeply upset by this biased use of my book, and at times found myself filled with anger at myself for losing control of my emotions when I wrote it. "It's too late to correct this," Kazem told me reprovingly. Correct what? Everything in the book is undeniable fact, but at the time of its writing I couldn't possibly have taken into account that it would be used against my intentions. I was helpless in the face of the rising tide. I ground my teeth and immersed myself in work and research.

It was during this period that I got Jane's letter announcing her marriage to Larry Davis. "He is two years younger than me," she wrote, "and I'm happy that Jimmy likes him." This letter caused me an emotional upheaval the likes of which I hadn't felt since the day she wrote that, for her, I would remain Jimmy's father. Indeed, the separation endured, and divorce gave it a legal stamp, but the fact that she would be with another man from now on, bear his name, and maybe even give my son that name too, confirmed my final expulsion from her life. For two days I felt shattered. Only after I told Kazem, and he said "Did you want her to stay alone?" Only then did I realize how selfish my reaction had been, and I rushed to send her my congratulations.

Assad was the second person to hear about it. I went to see him at the Ministry of Defense, where he had been posted after graduating from the officers training corps with the rank of lieutenant. He'd become thinner and brown from the sun, but he seemed comfortable in his new uniform. I saluted him as I came into his room;

he stood up, saluting back, and we both burst out laughing. "They badgered us well, but I don't regret it," he said.

I told him the uniform becomes him, and he replied: "But I don't become it."

He then told me it had been decided to post him to General Headquarters for the three months of compulsory service, as an editor of instructional material and English translator.

"An editor remains an editor," I said.

"This too shall pass," he replied. "Anyway, apart from night duty twice a week as commander of the guard, I can come home every night."

"Jane got married," I announced, without a preface.

He looked surprised, not only at the content of the announcement, but at the way I had switched to talk of my personal affairs. "I wish her all the best," he said after a short pause.

"I'll pass on your blessing," I said, "I'm sure she'll be glad."

A pensive smile spread over his face. He must have found this conversation peculiar, as did I. "She appreciates you, and likes you," I added.

"I do too. And Jamil?"

"She writes that he's on good terms with her husband."

"That's the most important thing."

"She married a pilot," I continued, with an urge to shake him out of his composure.

"A pilot? In the military?"

"She didn't say."

"I suppose she also didn't happen to mention whether he was Jewish?"

I expected this. One might even say I had asked for it, had made him pose this question, as illogical as this might seem.

We didn't talk much longer. As I stood up to leave I invited him to repay me with a visit at the office. He promised, but never came.

I CAN'T REMEMBER THE date, but it was after the British expeditionary forces were pulled out of Dunkirk and Hitler's attack on the Soviet Union, when a long poem by Assad Nissim was published in *al-Iraq*, titled "The New Order." This poem, as the paper reported, was first broadcast on BBC, and served as a reply of sorts to the Nazi propaganda directed by Yunas Bahri on Radio Berlin. I saw the publication of the poem as an opportunity to call him and commend him for his courage. "It's my humble contribution to the struggle against the Nazis," he said. I didn't repeat my invitation, but his visit was made possible without my initiative, when a problem arose regarding a construction plan by the Rafidayin textile company whose counsel he was. What he had to sort out wasn't my responsibility, but having come to City Hall, he saw fit to visit my office.

Four years had passed since the angry visit that marked the beginning of our break, and on coming in he stood and looked about, as if trying to assess whether something had changed in the room. "Nothing's changed, we haven't either," I told him.

"Yes? You think so?" He eyed me with wonder.

I ignored the charged tone of his voice and told him I was very happy to see him and talk to him, as a friend talks to a friend. I reiterated my admiration for his poem, which I considered one of the best he ever wrote, and added that it would be remembered a long time for the humanist spirit that echoed through its lines. I told him it was one of those universal poems that speak to all peoples struggling for liberty, fighting against tyranny.

Assad listened, his eyes avoiding mine, a reserved and introverted smile on his face; when I was done, there was a silence. "I don't want you to think I'm indifferent to what's going on around us," I said, trying to get him to talk.

"And why would I think you're indifferent?" He replied with a question.

"You're angry at me, Assad," I kept trying to get him to talk.

"If that's how you feel, I can't change it."

"I want to know how you feel," I insisted.

"How I feel?" He turned sharply toward me, "I feel sorry for you, that's all. I wouldn't want to be in your place, I wouldn't wish it upon any friend to be in your place."

"Why don't you also say you're mad at me?" I asked.

"No, I'm not mad. If I were, I wouldn't have come to ask you for an explanation."

"If that's how it is, you should know I have no regrets."

"That's your business," he said, his arm swaying.

"I don't regret a word I wrote either," I continued. "I'm just not happy that my words were taken out of context and my intentions distorted."

He didn't respond. Instead, he told me about a leaflet given to him to edit during his service, it was used to teach literacy to soldiers and contained a passage in garbled Arabic under the heading "No Trust in the Jews." He refused to edit the leaflet, and gave it back to the officer in charge of education. The officer, unaware of its content, marked the leaflet "not for publication".

"This is what you say to me after what I just told you?" I asked.

"And what did you expect? Since you don't regret a word you wrote."

"You talk to me with such condescension," I raised my voice, "as if we hadn't already talked about all this after Reuben's scandal, as if you didn't agree with all my arguments. And what did I write? Did I write anything different? But you don't want to admit it, all you care about is that the words are on paper!"

"Because words on paper are quoted."

"Good. Finally you admit that's the only difference between us!"

"Not just that," he replied, startling me. "The difference is that I'm a Jew and you're a convert!"

He used the derogatory Hebrew word, *meshumad*, connoting apostasy and treachery, and for that moment, for just that moment, I saw him as an enemy. I stood up briskly. "If that's how you see me, we better end this conversation," I said, and I meant it.

Assad gave me a quizzical and somewhat amused look: "What's shocking to you? Did I say something inaccurate?"

"You just hate me," I yelled.

"No, I have no reason to hate you. You asked, and I answered." He crossed his feet and leaned back in his chair, signaling to me that he had no intention of leaving.

"Curses are not what I expected from you," I replied, and sat down again.

"Listen to a story," he said, his voice indifferent to my protest. "You know I'm no big expert on Judaism, in fact, you're the expert. But listen to something you might not be aware of." He told me that the chief rabbi used to pose questions to visitors not only to test them, but mainly to teach them. In one of his meetings with the rabbi, a visitor asked if he knew who Aher, the Outcast, was. Since he didn't know, the rabbi told him the story of Elisha Ben Abuya, a brilliant rabbinic authority at the time of the *Mishna*, who was captivated by Greek philosophy and studied the science of mathematics until finally his faith in the god of Israel faltered and he found himself fleeing to Antioch. "This man preached the assimilation of the Jews among the Romans," he concluded. "He put himself at the service of Rome, and even informed on his former friends during the Bar-Kochba rebellion."

"This is what his enemies among the zealots alleged," I said.

"You know the story?" he asked.

"And I know why you're telling me this story," I replied.

"So we understand each other." He stood up, with a victorious smile.

"I'd hoped not to find you among the zealots," I said emphatically.

"You're wrong. If I were with the zealots I'd be mad at you. I told you I harbor no anger toward you, only sorrow."

We parted with a handshake. About a month later the Rashid 'Ali Kilani coup took place.

KAZEM IS DEAD. For two weeks he lay unconscious. My dear friend, a soul mate, has departed. The funeral is tomorrow.

THE HEADLINES DO NOT forebode well. Every day the leaders of the Iranian revolution reveal their true face. It's become clear that they hate Iraq even more than they hated the Shah and his regime. This hatred now bursts out in all its ugliness, with no restraint. The masses riot and the government eggs them on them with venomous tirades against Iraq and its president. A bomb thrown at the embassy in Teheran, arrests among Iraqi subjects, and incitement for the Kurds in the north to revolt against the Ba'athist regime. God has graced Kazem by saving him such bitter disappointment.

I think of him and cry. I couldn't control myself when I was asked to say some words in his memory at the funeral. The tears choked me. He had great expectations from the Islamic Revolution and was truly concerned by Khomeini's expulsion, an event he tried hard to understand. This expulsion was a cause of concern for all of us, no less than our concern for the man's inexcusable activities among the Shi'ites. All this should have been treated with some wisdom, to avoid a confrontation and a breach with the leaders of the revolution. Kazem was saved from such disappointment. Throughout, he remained a man of faith.

I think of him constantly, and talk to him at length. I miss him so much in these days of turmoil. He was a man who knew the right word for the right time. I came to know him in this way—in my bewildered days he gave me support and revived my spirit. "Your turn to Islam is as pure as the conversion of the righteous men, the Prophet's companions. You didn't inherit it, nor were you influenced by preaching, but arrived at it out of study and contemplation." Those were his words to me when I came back from Cairo, and that is what he wrote about my book. I shared my deliberations with him, and he never tried to turn my heart this way or that; moreover, he warned me that my decision might be interpreted maliciously. When he received the published version of the book, he couldn't conceal his astonishment at the additions to the chapters on contemporary Judaism. He had found no fault in the original manuscript I sent from Cairo, before I added those passages, and so he took me to task for using such harsh language against the Jews, finding the material displeasing. "This is redundant," he told me. "You shouldn't have let yourself get carried away with emotions that have no place in a serious book." I asked if he'd met Assad and he replied: "I respect Assad Nissim," and nothing more.

I find it hard to write about Kazem. He always stood by my side, and his advice helped show me the way. I had reservations about his criticism, and only later did I grasp how apt it was. My temperament outpaced me, I saw Reuben before me when I wrote what I did about the Jews as human beings. Later I felt a deep regret for the way those words were used by people I hadn't taken into account. He was wise and decent, and when I think of the years I lived in his company, it is clear to me that our friendship was made up of generosity and giving on his side, with no reciprocation from me. He wanted nothing in exchange.

AZIZ LAHAM IS FILTH personified. He turned up drunk at the mourning gathering, and with no manners or respect for the deceased, annoyed us with his lunatic attacks on the Sh'ia, the *shari'a*, and the Islamic Revolution. Khomeini's supporters in Iraq, he said, are a fifth column and must be put down mercilessly. And the *shari'a*, championed by the leaders of the Islamic Revolution in Iran, as well as by the "*brethren*" in Egypt and Syria and their followers in Iraq, is nothing but a barbaric law, unworthy of civilized society. His face puffy and his eyes bloodshot, he sat silent and distant for half an hour, then suddenly took a folded leaflet out of his pocket and presented it to us as the agenda of the Islamic Movement. From that moment on, no one could interrupt his rambling speech and every comment, no matter how gentle, only incited him more. I wish I'd gotten up and left when he came. I would have saved myself some unnecessary excitement. I did my best not to look at him and not to respond to his words, but he wouldn't let me be. While reading from the leaflet, written by one of the "*brethren*" in Syria, he made a point of addressing me directly.

The thrust of his attack was dedicated to passages regarding "protected subjects" in the Islamic state. "Some of us long for a *shari'a* state," he said, eyeing me. "They want to implement that barbaric law that divides the world in two: Muslims and infidels. Whoever is not a Muslim is an infidel, to be humiliated, and must acknowledge the superiority of Islam, and be the first to greet a Muslim. The protected subjects won't have the right to be elected to parliament, to hold a government position, or even to chair a meeting. It's all written here, in black and white!"

His words were an obvious provocation to everyone present, and I knew he expected some response from me to make me an easy target for his attacks. Did he bring the leaflet with him on the assumption that he would find me there? Would he have been more restrained had I not been there? I think it was all planned. He acted like an informant, not like someone presenting a real critique or expressing a dislike for the models he referred to. He wasn't speaking under the influence either, but alcohol did set his tongue loose. And he had no qualms about carrying out his despicable job at a gathering of mourners. I believe most of those present reached this conclusion on their own since, after a few initial words of protest, no one even bothered to interrupt him. Only the entry of a few neighbors shut him up for some reason, and he resumed his distant gaze. A short while later I stood up to say my good-byes to the family members. I was surprised when he caught up with me by the door. "I'll accompany you," he said with a malevolent smile.

"I've heard enough from you," I said and turned to go.

He grabbed my arm. "I have more to say to you. That much I promised you!"

"You're drunk," I pulled my arm free of his grasp.

"But you'll still listen to me," his tall figure blocked my path. "Your conscience haunts you."

"My conscience or yours, for behaving this way at a wake?"

"Zuhair weighs on your conscience. He is your victim. A foolish follower of this Islamic Revolution of yours and Kazem's!"

I was outraged. "How dare you blame Kazem?"

"You're a dangerous gang, and you, personally, are the most dangerous!"

His aggression was unbearable, and I decided to put him in his place. "A man like you should be ashamed," I told him. "You have no right to blame others, and if you had even a shred of self respect you wouldn't show yourself in public."

"Only a man like me can tell you the truth about yourself," he replied bluntly. "For I've been through hell and know the true nature of those who speak of justice and revolution. None of them is clean. They're all dirty, and the communists more than anyone. Your friend Qassem is just like them."

"It's you who is filthy," I said, trembling.

"We're all filthy, Haroun." he lowered his voice, like one just making conversation. "We are all alike and there are no saints among us, but you are a hypocrite too!"

I didn't know how to get away from him. He stood in front of me and blocked my passage, arousing the curiosity of passers by. "Leave me alone," I told him, overcoming my anger, but he nodded: "When you hear my question. Why did you leave *My Path to Islam* off your list of publications? You appended a long list of publications to your book, forgetting only your first book. Why?"

"I'll answer you another time, not now, not on the street," I replied in an effort to please him and end the embarrassing spectacle.

"I don't need your answer," he raised his voice, his lips forming a venomous smile. "You think readers are stupid and don't know who you are? Your call for a jihad against the Jews brings a shame upon our heads that we've never witnessed before in history!"

I cried out at him that he was a crazy drunkard, but he grabbed both my arms and filled my face with his smelly breath: "You're a Jewish impersonator," he thundered, and began emitting his wretched laughter.

I almost ran to get away from him. I can't unwind. How dare he? Before you know it, he'll accuse me of being a Zionist agent!

RIGHT AWAY BUTHEINA SAW that I wasn't feeling well. I was sitting in the big chair with my head laid back when she came in, Sarah at her heels. "Everything is alright," I told her, and called Sarah to show me a new toy her father had given her.

Butheina put her hand on my forehead. "You're pale. Did you take your nitro?" And before I could answer she took the pills out of the desk drawer and handed me one. "Grandfather is tired," she pulled Sarah away from me. "Go to Grandma now."

I had to tell her I had an annoying talk with Aziz Laham, and that he had disgraced himself in Kazem's house. I didn't tell her what he had said to me, nor would I even have had time to before Hamida burst into the room:

"What's the matter? What happened?"

"Nothing happened, Mother," Butheina replied. "Father is a bit tired, that's all."

"Tired? Did you give him a pill?"

"I did. He's better now."

"You think I can't see? It's been a week already that he looks like a shadow, he can't even sleep at night. I'll call the doctor!"

She rushed to the phone, in spite of my objection. Nothing could stop her. Dr. Hikmat arrived half an hour later and found no cause for worry. "A little rest and it will go away," he told Hamida who tracked every move of his examination suspiciously.

"Give him something for sleep," she said.

But he saw no reason to change the sleeping pills he himself had already prescribed. "Take two, a half hour after dinner," he told me.

I did as he said, and was in bed by nine-thirty. I fell into a deep sleep and woke up at five. I stayed in the room until Hamida got up.

HAD AZIZ LAHAM KNOWN who suggested that I not include *My Path to Islam* in my list of publications, he might not have said what he did. I thought of asking Takriti to shut him up but decided the better of it when I remembered how he reacted to my thoughts about Zuhair. For the time being Aziz is a tool in their hands, and I shouldn't bestow any undeserved importance upon him. It's Friday and Butheina is at home. I had tea in the kitchen with her and told Sarah the story of the Flying Dutchman. She was so entranced by the story that she finished her bowl of porridge without even realizing she'd been distracted. Then she clapped her hands at her own achievement as her mother called out: "What a sweet girl ate up her porridge!"

"I propose you sit with her every morning," she told me later.

"That would be the best thing he could do," Hamida joined in.

Butheina started to laugh, bringing up lullabies I sang to her when she was a child, the ones I could still remember from my own childhood. "They were sad songs you sang to me," she said, "but I loved them."

"You were a big cry baby," Hamida told her.

"I went way up high / To chill water in the wind / But the wind knocked me over / And that's how my / pitcher got broken," Butheina chanted and laughed. "Such a sad song, I used to feel sorry for the poor girl and the broken pitcher."

"Your mother sang prettier songs for you," I said.

"Yours were beautiful too," she put her arm around my head and kissed me. "You're the best father in the world!"

At ten a friend came to see her, a Sumeriologist, and I was asked to join them for a little while. It was pleasant to discuss my favorite subjects with a guest and, in particular, to explain some issues I touched upon both in *The Jews in History* and *Studies in Arab Civilization*, the book that came out two years ago. The guest had some questions to pose and one of them was about our common practice of making vows to Khidr. In my book I had pointed out, without elaborating on it much, that this was the remnant of an ancient custom that could be traced to the Sumerians. I told her this popular belief had been given various interpretations, all of them erroneous, for the simple reason that we refer to Khidr as Khidr Elias. The custom of lighting a candle on a piece of wood or on the base of a palm branch, on the first of every month, and floating it on the water, originates from the Sumerian myth of Enki since, according to the story, should the candle stop burning and disappear, it would be a sign that Khidr had accepted the plea of the supplicant standing on the river bank. In popular belief, I said, Khidr had identical attributes to the Sumerian god of fertility that dwells in the waters of the holy Euphrates, and it was no mere coincidence that belief in Khidr and fables about him were especially common among fresh water sailors and fishermen. But some scholars, Jews in particular, try to connect Elias with Elijah, known in Jewish fables as a prophet and miracle-worker. These scholars rely, among other things, on another Muslim fable, about Moses' travel to the Majma' Bahrain, the confluence of the Tigris and the Euphrates, where he met Khidr as a man in a green coat that lay on the shore. Khidr took Moses aboard a ship and put him through three trials to test his endurance but Moses failed the trials and so realized that this was no ordinary human but one of god's angels. This fable has nothing to do with the myths of Elijah, who was not a man of water, it comes from Sumerian civilization and the myths of Enki, whereas the name Elias attached by people to Khidr's name is a much later addition that shouldn't mislead us.

I am fond of Mesopotamian history and was very happy to speak to the young scholar. Had I chosen the academic path I'm sure I'd have turned to the study of the ancient world and forsaken my specialization in international relations. But for this I'd have had to stay in America as there was no university in Iraq and teaching at the high college for teachers or at the law school didn't appeal to me. I stayed an engineer and my love of history was put aside. An amateur historian. That's what I am, and that's the way professional historians see me. And the Jewish orientalist from France could afford to insult me. I hear you are an engineer. Yes, and what does being an engineer have to do with researching the history of the Jews? That's how they are. Dominating every field. Oriental studies, science, rewriting the history of the Arabs. They cut Mesopotamian civilization off from the indigenous people, as if other peoples had created it, and not the inhabitants of this fertile valley. Conveniently they deny the Arabs any originality and talk of their civilization as a desert culture that adopted the culture of peoples conquered under the banner of Islam. The Jews, and their allies among Christian scholars, insist on the bible as a historical source without leaving the Arabs and Islam any function beyond the absorption of influences from Judaism and Christianity, Persia and Greece. But the most tragic part of it is that we have accepted these assumptions as unquestionable truisms and rendered ourselves rootless in the very land we inhabit. It was convenient for us too, to adopt these assumptions in order to advance the Muslim Arab identity, and to revise our history into a book making its debut with the *jahiliya*, the time of ignorance, and the beginning of Islam. All that had preceded this does not belong. It's the history, supposedly, of other peoples, of bygone pagans. We have lied to ourselves, for Islam has no need to distort history, it did not emerge out of nothing, as the Quran testifies!

The study of Arab history requires a thorough revision, and no one can do this but us. This is what I have been writing for some fifteen years, and my last book proves how biased the claim of the originality and holiness of the Bible is. The Jews took whatever they could lay their hands on, from the myths of Sumer, Akkad, Canaan, Babylon, and Egypt, and attributed everything to themselves replete with extravagant distortions. And the Christian world followed suit and appropriated this great loot. Judeo-Christian civilization, they said, whereas we, descendants of ancient Eastern civilizations, were all considered rabble vanquished by the desert people. Rooting this lie out of Christian consciousness is an arduous task, it's hard to change Christian consciousness about the history of the Jews and their right to Palestine. If the English edition of my book will help our battle over minds, that would be reward enough for me.

"No one in the entire Arab world is as learned as you on the history of the Jews, so we rely on you," the Minister of Information told me. He referred me to Maulud Tikriti who provided me with two assistants and a secretary to collect the material and edit it.

Without them, I wouldn't have been able to complete the book in two years.

The Jews in History is a commissioned book, although I had contemplated writing it for a long time. I am proud the commission was assigned to me and no one else. In writing this book, I paid an old debt to the society that took me in. *My Path to Islam* was just a personal entry certificate, but this book is focused on the general national motivation, not the personal. And I have to admit here, it was not I, but Tikriti, who suggested the omission of my first book from the list of publications. I accepted his proposal without hesitation and even asked that the press not offer any hint of my Jewish origin. This is the truth, and I put it down here, just as I have put down Aziz Laham's foul words.

But can I ignore his outburst? Even if I didn't care less about his allegations, neither I nor any responsible person could disregard the quote he read from the "brethren's" leaflet. The danger is real, and if we don't deal with it, we're going to face gory civil wars. My book is a small contribution to our information campaign, it fulfills an inferred mission against an enemy whose power is like that of a super power. But neither I nor my generation are qualified for this great and crucial task, it is up to the younger generation to reread history. This generation will have to be critical not only of the west but, also, and in particular, of the Arab–Muslim historiography that has systematically erased the history of peoples that have espoused Islam and eradicated the glory of their ancestors for hundreds of years. Indeed, a different political climate is needed to execute this task, an enlightened Islamic climate, something so far and such a great distance from us.

IT'S A PLEASURE TO hear Butheina talk with Jamil on the phone. He called to ask about Sabry and there wasn't really anything I could tell him, nor did I want to speak of him at length. When Butheina took the phone their conversation flowed with the excitement that only caring, loving siblings can express. The tight bond they formed since meeting next to Jane's grave is a godsend. "My little sister," Jamil called her, and still does. "Is my little sister home?" he asked.

What did I contribute to this connection? Nothing. Till the age of six Butheina didn't even know she had a brother in America and she would surely have remained unaware of it for years if it hadn't been for that sad incident when she came home from school all in tears. "The Jew's daughter," that's what an envious girl had called her, and the entire class began harassing her. Hamida sat her in her lap and told her what she didn't know about her father, and on my return home she looked at me suspiciously and tried to avoid approaching me. The year was 1951, the whole city was talking of the Jewish exodus, and they found it in their heads to inform that menace of a girl that the object of her envy had a Jewish father. I sat her on my knees and talked to her at length of myself, of Jane, and of Jamil. I showed her his pictures, kept in a special album, including some Jane took of him in my company during my visit in 1948. She regained her composure, and laughter lit up her face again. That night I called the school principal and reminded her of her responsibility to prevent such behavior from ever recurring. She was embarrassed, apologized, and on the next day acted commendably. She summoned the envious girl's parents for an urgent talk, then visited the class and talked to the girls about Butheina's father, his stature, and his contribution to the homeland. Butheina was happy to hear the principal speak of her father that way, and since then she knew how to defend herself when anyone so much as tried to insinuate anything, as children do to tease one another.

A child ashamed of their parents is an unhappy child. Butheina was not ashamed of me, but she bore me a grudge. She didn't ask about Jamil again and whenever his name came up in conversation with Hamida she'd wrap herself in silence or get busy with something. The subject was taboo for her and she protected herself by acting as if it didn't matter, although it had quite the opposite effect on her. I noted this with disquiet and all I could do was hire a private English tutor for her, hoping that when the time came she'd be able to speak freely to her brother. Jamil was twenty-six when she met him, an electrical engineer making his way into business, and she was only thirteen. I asked her if she was pleased to know her brother, and she nodded and gave me one of her wise looks that made words superfluous. I tried to use tender language to tell her that from now on she could be proud of having a handsome older brother with whom she could exchange letters and of whom she can tell her friends, not realizing I hit a sore spot. "Jamil is an orphan," she burst out in tormented weeping. "He has no mother and no father either!"

What truth she spoke! She made me face my own image. Jamil, my firstborn son, was he not bereft of a father during all these years? Was I not worthy of Butheina's contempt? She bore me a grudge ever since that incident at school, and let it all out seven years later, leaving me in shame. But I was wrong to think that was the end of it. A child's grudge against their father is not easily disposed of, and I was to be embarrassed again.

Today I enjoy hearing her talk to her brother, I'm happy about his friendship with Sabry, but my heart is heavy. Jane is gone, Butheina is divorced, and Sarah will grow up without a father, like Jamil, and I never see Jamil's three sons.

IN THESE PAGES I am trying to deliver the facts accurately. It isn't my life story I'm telling, I'm only trying to give an honest report of experiences and situations as they come up in my consciousness, as I best remember them. Actually, I am making a confession, so I'll try not to summarize and draw conclusions. For what compelled me to write is the desire to serve witness about myself and my times, a personal testimony, based solely on my own perspective which, I believe, doesn't lack originality. I've published profusely during my days on earth, books and articles, but as opposed to everything I wrote so far this is not aimed at a particular reader, nor do I have the faintest notion whether a reader for this will be found or what the times might be like when that comes to pass. I could have claimed I'm writing for myself but that wouldn't be true, for a man doesn't write to himself alone, even if the urge to write is the urge to document experience for one's own personal use. I've read many personal journals and purportedly intimate memoirs by authors and statesmen published during their lifetimes or posthumously, and I always wondered: these people who wrote what they did in different times, did they not imagine a day would come when their personal journals would be made public? If that was the case, they didn't write for themselves alone and, by sharing their experiences with the paper, they had taken them out of hiding in the privacy of their minds. An intimate journal has its own form of being and nothing exists, whether a living being or still pages, that isn't communicative, that has no destiny beyond the circle of privacy, beyond the circle of time and place.

I could say I am writing this not in order to publish it, but in the hope it will be published. And another thing: I know these pages will have one sure reader, Butheina, my daughter. That is to say, I am depositing my self portrait with her, and she can do with it as she likes. The authors of memoirs who, like me, approach such writing in their old age—after getting their publicity and attaining their high positions—tend to be self-congratulatory, showing others how they overcame difficulties, what lessons might be drawn, and how to climb to the peak after being down and out. That isn't what engages me. I am writing of a life experience in which neither failure nor success is at issue, rather, what is at stake is experience itself.

I already mentioned how much I wanted to join the diplomatic corps. Politics attracted me, and I was confident I could be of more help to my country than any regular politician. In those days a politician was someone whose virtues were trickery and deceit, whose aspiration was to dominate and gain benefits for himself and those under his patronage. I was naïve to think my path was blocked merely because of being Jewish; the path was blocked to anyone without a gang of supporters backing them, anyone lacking "electoral power" according to prevalent tribal concepts. Iraq was a country of competing tribes, and much blood was shed over insignificant disputes. Someone buying off a tribe or getting backed by another could become hero, threaten to riot, shake up the government, become a member of parliament or a minister. The British regime manipulated the tribal medley according to its needs, turning one camp against another, inciting disputes between Shi'ites and Sunnis, between Arabs and Kurds, even setting its own gang of cronies against each other to make them grovel. The Bakr Sidqi coup might have been a turning point, but it was corrupted and collapsed into ethnic fighting. I realized, with much regret, that in this theater of opposing camps a man like me had no foothold.

Sadness has many facets; the worst, in my view, is related to supposedly fleeting, unimportant acts. You regret a silly act that annoyed your parents—offending a classmate, some slip of the tongue, minute details that are supposed to be forgotten and disappear, but remain deeply engraved in your consciousness, and whenever you bring them up an unpleasant sense of contempt overtakes you. I feel that way when I recall my foolish attempt to get elected to parliament. The war years were a time of fervent political activity. The British had an interest in blunting public hostility toward them by allowing liberal circles and the left to act freely, aiming to bring about public endorsement for the allies against support for the Axis Powers. At that time political ambitions came back to taunt me. I sympathized with Kamel al-Chadarchi's National Democratic party but couldn't join and was disinclined to become a member of any party. Yet, I was close to Shi'ite circles, and through Kazem, whom I used to meet at the Zahawi Cafe for a round of backgammon, I became privy to a group of activists affiliated with Saleh Jabr who was to enter the history books after signing the Portsmouth Treaty with Britain in 1948. In truth, I had some sympathy for the Shi'ites to begin with, as the disenfranchised, not to mention that I grew up among them, and naturally felt part of the Ja'afri school of thought, adhered to by my townsmen. That same Shi'ite group that was one day to become the party, established a non-ethnic image by taking Sunnis and even Christians into its ranks. Thus, in 1946, I was toying with the notion of getting elected to parliament.

But to transform that abstract notion into a decision to announce my candidacy in the Hila district, a chance meeting with the Prince Regent, 'Abed Ilaah was needed. That year Umm Kulthum came to sing in the Rihab Palace, the Prince Regent's palace, as part of the annual Coronation Day celebration. I was invited to this festive soiree, and during one of the intermissions stopped for a cold drink at the bar where the master of ceremonies approached me and said the Prince Regent was calling me. I turned back and saw 'Abd Ilaah standing in the company of Saleh Jabr and two or three government ministers, looking at me and smiling. I was surprised, and confused. When I stepped toward him he preceded my greeting with a question: "How are you, Doctor?" He then said: "We hear good things about you." I replied that I do what I can for the good of the homeland. "Saleh has told me about you," he continued, turning to Jabr who nodded in confirmation.

That short conversation clarified something that I had not seen quite as clearly before, namely, that the Prince Regent, who always tried to maintain an equilibrium between opposing groups in support of Britain, wanted to see Saleh Jabr become stronger, to pose a counter balance for Nuri Sa'id, the strong man in the government. But more than anything, this conversation taught me that the Crown Prince considered my election to parliament of importance, and he hoped to see me take on some official responsibility. After my disappointment in 1936, I was happy to find out the government wanted to mend its ways and seek the help of people like me, whose strength lay not in a camp of adherents, but in their faculties. But the more I thought of this the more I worried: On what principles was I to base my platform? And how could I make it known to the public? I wasn't anonymous amongst my constituency but hadn't been in touch with them for years; moreover, when they knew me, I was a Jew! "All this is unimportant," Kazem told me. "You should be satisfied that the regime wants you and approaches you, that you are not forcing yourself on the regime."

I felt I was dreaming, gaining such high recognition made me seem even more grand. For this was what I had aspired to all along: to be accepted, to be found trustworthy, not only on a professional level, but on a wider national level! However, the euphoria was short-lived, and ended in disappointment. My opponent in the constituency was an ignorant man from the Busultan tribe, a clan of important lineage and power, and when I expressed my hesitation I was told: Your election is certain, it's all been arranged, you'll be elected by *tazkiya*, without an actual vote. I felt as though they had spat in my face. They intended to place me in parliament using the same despicable scheme of mobilizing tribes by bribery and the promise of benefits, and in my stupidity, in my ambition, I lent my hand to this and collaborated!

This was my last attempt to enter politics. I came out unharmed, my reputation undamaged, but whenever I think of the situation I might have found myself in, I'm bathed in a cold sweat. The elected parliament was one of the most corrupt in the history of Iraq, and on its very first session the elected representatives of the National Democratic Party announced their resignation to protest against the fixed elections. The parliament was meant to ratify the contract secretly signed with Britain, when Saleh Jabr had appointed his government and aroused the 1948 insurrection.

A single mistake can lead a man to disaster, and escaping it just in time leaves one with a painful, frustrating sediment, but there are other situations in which a man finds himself in trouble through no fault of his own, and the memory of it never fades.

IF MY BOOK *The Jews in History* should come into Assad's hands, I'm sure he'd remember our conversation of March or April 1941. Perhaps the book might even move him to break his silence about our friendship and our disagreement, something he might dedicate a chapter to in his memoirs. I hope his memory doesn't fail him, and the trumpets of Zionist propaganda don't force him to pervert the truth. But he wouldn't write of me with affection, the way I've written about him; he wouldn't be able to write about me sympathetically even if nothing were required of him, for he has an account to settle with me, and my account is with Judaism. He sees me as a deserter, a traitor and an informer; indeed, he told me as much in his own way — is there any reason for him to change his mind, now that he lives in the Zionist state? To each his truth, to each his half of the glass.

I told him I didn't regret one word I wrote, to make him remove this mask of indifference and force him to open his heart to me. I most certainly had no regrets, what got to me then was the use that was made of my book — it wasn't to my liking and went against my intentions. I couldn't demand not to be quoted, and I was afraid to react to things published in my name lest I turn myself into a sitting duck. A Jew who converts is always suspicious, even more so when he tries to defend Jews. At the time I was more troubled by the hateful language used to attack the Jews, the sort of language I condemned in my book, but for its prevalent use by Judaism against gentiles. I chose Islam out of the will to extract myself from the chains of separatism and couldn't bear to see myself escaping Jewish xenophobia and zealousness only to fall into the hands of Muslim zealots and xenophobes. I was helpless, like one robbed of his own personality, and this burning insult tormented me.

But the insult was nothing compared to the depression that engulfed me during the two days of the *farhud*. I sat in the city's nerve center and anxiously followed reports of murder and the looting of Jewish homes as they arrived. I do not aim to analyze the situation in Baghdad after the Kilani uprising was squelched and the Prince Regent returned to the palace. Nor will I touch upon the controversy as to why the British army didn't enter the city, even after it had defeated the forces supporting the government of the uprising. Much research has already been dedicated to this, and many versions of these events have been collected. I am writing about myself, about the Jew in me, about the loneliest person in the city during those two days of rioting.

I listened to my colleagues' talk blaming the British for inciting the riots, I heard them complain of the helplessness of the police, of soldiers taking part in the looting. I asked myself: What am I doing here? What is my place? The Mayor called me to his office and asked if I wanted anything. "Give me addresses and I'll send armed supervisors." I didn't have addresses. I knew my brother lived in Sinak, and my sister Na'ima in Taht-al-Takia. My other two sisters didn't live in Baghdad. "My hands are tied," he told me. "There's no hope of stopping the riots without military intervention, and I have no control over the army!" I didn't reply. I was petrified. Finally I remembered Assad, and called him. Assad has been called up to the army, his wife said. She was worried, but the neighborhood had been quiet thus far. The Mayor looked at me and I let out a nervous laugh. How absurd! The Jewish officer guards the state, and the citizens of the state persecute the Jews! "I'll send a guard to your place," the Mayor promised before hanging up. "I don't trust the police," he later told me, "but the supervisors are my men and if one of them is caught helping the rioters I'll hang him with my own two hands!"

He slapped his hand on the table, as if to affirm what he said. I felt sorry for him. I felt even sorrier for him two days later, when he stood ignominiously, asking forgiveness from groups of Jews who came to complain to him.

Reuben wasn't hurt but in Taht-al-Takia and in the other Jewish neighborhoods people were killed, houses looted, and the honor of women violated. I was worried about Na'ima and sent Sha'aban to look for her house. My heart told me that she, the good sister who had violated Reuben's commandments and stayed in touch with me throughout the boycott, she of all people would be among the casualties. Sha'aban came back downcast. "Praise be to god, they are all well," he hastened to tell me. They escaped through the roofs, from one house to the next, soldiers among the rioters shot at those who ran away but they were saved; of their property, all they were left with were the clothes on their backs. "When I told her who sent me, she began to wail, and to beat her own face. The kids were scared." I couldn't hear him out. I rushed to my room and let myself go. I was lonely in my grief, alone and humiliated. With my own eyes I had seen the looters hurry down the streets and alleys carrying their spoils, I had heard their voices, their festive singing; I saw my neighbors rush to conceal the loot from my view, closing their doors when I passed by, or standing in their doorway and eyeing me obsequiously. I saw a city struck by madness and heard hair raising stories about cruel acts of rape and murder, of an outburst of dark urges, of humans who became beasts. I was in a state of shock, as if my senses were paralyzed, deprived of the power of judgment and thought. The news Sha'aban brought had the effect of melting at once all that had been frozen, and whenever I remembered that my sister and her daughters might have fallen victims to rape, I was overtaken by a spasm of sobbing.

On that day I fully comprehended the tragic meaning of being other. It was as if Assad had foreseen the situation I'd find myself in. That horrid isolation, that cut off. I cried. I felt no regret, but a razor sharp sense of self-awareness. I'll be different forever, lonely forever, other forever.

I kept thinking about what I could do for my sister. It did cross my mind to visit her in person, but I couldn't predict her husband's reaction, or that of her neighbors. The municipality began recording victims' complaints, sending supervisors and policemen to retrieve the stolen property and return it to its owners. The government decided to compensate victims with money, and in the mean time some of the rioters were arrested and put on trial. Some were executed by hanging.

I decided to send Na'ima a check for one thousand dinar, a very large sum in those days, and way beyond my means, but I wanted to somehow express my affection for her, and my gratitude to her for serving as my mother's mouth during the hard times. Sha'aban told me she was surprised by the check, muttered some words of gratitude, and asked how I was. I was overwhelmed with joy. I appeased my conscience by thinking I did the right thing. But the next day, to my grave disappointment, I found the envelope containing the check on my desk. Someone delivered it, they told me, but could not tell me who.

IT WAS STRANGE TO convene the preparatory committee for the Academy's 40th anniversary celebrations at such a grim, unfestive time. Arrests and expulsions of Iranian subjects and their supporters continue, while in Iran our missions have become the target of daily attacks by incited masses and our subjects are held humiliated, like hostages. Iraq's leaders are blamed for collaboration with the Shah's *Savak* and none other than Bani Sadr, the young president and graduate of the Sorbonne, announced an all-Islamic revolution to purge Iraq of infidels and enemies of Islam. We talked about the state of affairs more than the preparations. Jawad al-'Alawi was concerned by the arrests, and by the spread of rumors and informants, and Mahmoud al-Janabi said what many are saying these days, that it looks like there'll be war. But Moustafa al-Sharbati was, as always, the optimist. It won't be long, he said, before we discover the Zionists and the Americans behind Khomeini—it will be an international scandal, bigger than Watergate, but not a war. May this come true, although being an optimist these days strikes me as devoid of all reason.

Sabry is nervous. He accompanied Badriya to visit Zuhair. They wouldn't let him in so she went in alone, with a large group of visitors. She saw her son behind two rows of thick iron mesh, and as the whole crowd was yelling, she could barely hear his voice. She came back in tears and, in her confusion, forgot to leave the bundle she had prepared for him. "She's lost all hope," he told me. "The girls won't leave her on her own for a minute, they're afraid she'll do something desperate." She goes to see fortune tellers, takes vows, makes pilgrimage to the saints' tombs. Beautiful Badriya, Qassem's beloved, the woman to whom he was faithful his entire life, in whom he had awakened a rebellious spirit, thus will she be broken, this hardship will make her lose her mind. And Qassem in exile, how she longs for his confident voice, his robust faith, his prohibitions: Not to shed a tear, not to surrender, not to feel sorry for yourself!

I asked Sabry if he wasn't disappointed by the man he used to speak so highly of, now calling for jihad against Iraq, and he said he was under pressure by the zealots, and forced to pay them lip service. "I'm worried by the situation here," he added. "We're no better, all we have are worn out slogans to fill our mouths. They blame us for collaborating with Zionism and Imperialism, and we blame them for being the agents of Imperialism and Zionism!"

"We're also infidels, the way they see it," I said.

"I would have accepted this allegation willingly, if it were genuine, but it's a fraud. All our slogans are a fraud. Socialism, revolution, science, lies, lies, and in the mean time we make ready for war!"

I expressed the hope that war could still be avoided, and warned him again, as I had more times than I could count, about unnecessary talk in public places. He lit a cigarette and stayed quiet, as though in reflection. "I'm careful, don't worry," he finally muttered. "But how can one take all this and keep quiet!"

He sat there, his back bent, not looking at me. I knew he had something on his mind that he had to tell me. I felt his remark wasn't innocent and I decided not to beat around the bush but make him speak out. Indeed, when I told him that prudence doesn't mean repeating things he doesn't believe in, but that a man living in places like we did would do well to speak half the truth, or even one tenth of it, as long as he didn't draw the wrath of the government against him, he turned to me, surprised: "And is that what you do?"

"I don't do anything I don't believe in, and what I do is what's expected of me," I replied.

Sabry gave me a sharp, bitter look that made me admit I had little willingness to join the delegation in support of the President, but I didn't regret it either because what we want now is to prevent ethnic factions. I added that if support for the President was taken to mean support for the regime, this wouldn't be very far from the truth. We must pay the price in order to maintain stability. I also said that our mistake is not to present our own Islamic agenda against Khomeini's Islamic propaganda, one that wouldn't preach a return to historical standards, but be based on national, cultural, and moral concepts that could distinguish us from the Christian West.

"Being backward is what distinguishes us from the West," he replied.

"Backwardness is one thing, the other is our authentic identity, and that is Islam."

"Islam is backwardness," he drew heavily on his cigarette, and extinguished it nervously.

I told him that such talk wouldn't get us anywhere, and we had to face reality, not get caught in foreign ideologies that grew out of other societies in other times.

"But talking about Islamic ethics isn't ideological?" he replied sternly. "What ethics? Islam was soiled with blood from its very beginning. Three of the first four Caliphs were assassinated, and those who took power were the ones who fought against the Prophet, it was they who spread Islam by the might of the sword!" He straightened up and looked directly at me. "Will you be angry if I tell you something? An Islamic manifesto that talks of a modern secular state, isn't that a foreign ideology?"

"We take the principle of secularism from the West, that's true."

"But you talk of an authentic Muslim identity," he replied, his face flushed by the challenge. "That is, Islam is the foundation for a comprehensive national concept. This sort of reminds me of something. Excuse me, but I can just quote your own words about Zionism!"

I made him reveal what was in his heart. I wasn't angry, but surprised. If that's what he thinks, maybe Butheina thinks so too?

"There isn't a shred of semblance between Zionism, which sees Judaism as a nationality, and what I am saying," I responded curtly. And when he repeated his claim that Islam and secularism contradicted one another, I told him that anti-religious zealotry provoked religious zealotry, and we ought to be wary of that.

He didn't reply, and clearly preferred not to continue arguing. It was my preference too. "If we can't agree on this," I said after a short pause, "maybe we can reach agreement on something else."

"I know what you want," he burst out laughing in relief.

"That's the main point," I concluded, and took a bottle of whiskey from the sideboard.

I wanted to end this conversation in good humor because I knew I wasn't going to change his opinion of me and I didn't care if he thought I preached a distorted ideology or that I was a coward, writing what I'm asked to write and collaborating with a tyranny. I didn't even care if he said as much to Jamil. Just let him go, let him be on the outside, don't let him bring disaster upon us.

I THINK OF QASSEM. A seventy-seven year old exile in a country whose language he doesn't speak—how does he get through the day? Does he meet other exiles like himself? Blacks who fled the apartheid regime? Chinese refugees from Maoist rule, Arabs persecuted by military coups? Maybe, like me, he is writing his memoirs. A man who avoided speaking about himself his whole life, speaks to paper in his old age. He thought conversations that weren't about society and politics, imperialism and socialism, the worker or the peasant, were idle, wasteful conversations. He hid his feelings, and cloaked his moments of weakness under the cover of struggle—as for his relationship to Badriya, no one dared ask. When I think back on those times so many years ago in al-Hila, I can't seem to remember if he ever spoke about his parents, how he felt about them, or about his brothers, things that concerned kids back then, that also concerned Assad and me. When we talked about such things in his company, he kept quiet and seldom joined

171

the conversation. I was aware of his difference, and it was probably impossible not to be aware of it. We weren't like him, but his introversion didn't disturb us. We used to meet in the neighborhood and play, going out for walks along the banks of the river, sneaking into the cafes scattered around down there, listening in on the men talking. There was no sense of any difference between us, we swam against each other, ran races, hunted the wild doves and rode horses, always competing as equals. We recited the kinds of poetry they made us learn in school and, at Assad's house, we secretly read the tattered pages of a copy of *A Thousand And One Nights* that belonged to his older brother who had left for Baghdad. And when we parted, it was only natural to us that Assad and I returned to spacious houses, well laden tables, and clean beds, while Qassem went back to a dark hut where he slept in one room with his parents and siblings. Kids from the nice part of town didn't think about worldly matters and, according to them, class differences were the concern of grown-ups. Qassem saw things differently, from the perspective of the bottom of the ladder—his gaze was turned above while ours roamed about along the surface, along my horizon, naive and indolent. "I won't be a peasant and neither will you," he said, and he knew what he was saying.

I remember an editorial meeting of *al-Rassid* after the publication of his article about the new statutes regarding land ownership that had recently passed into law. This law, meant to settle disputes between landowners, actually was aimed at dispossessing the peasants from their land and turning them into serfs. The article was brilliant in its ability to analyze the situation, pointing not only to the injustice facilitated by the law, but also to the further repercussions of the law on the younger generation of peasants and the future of agriculture itself. As well might be expected, the article provoked the ire of one of the financial backers who warned Assad that articles of that sort were not covered under the permit granted for a literary journal and might lead to the publication's closure. We sat in Assad's office and talked it over. At some point I told Qassem that the best response to the backer's warning would be to publish another article describing the difficult conditions of his schooling, and all the obstacles he had to overcome to get where he is. Assad was all for it, saying it would make a gripping story, but Qassem vehemently rejected the idea. "I won't tell any gripping stories to the enemy."

"Readers are the enemy?" I asked.

"The enemy is interested in stories like that so they can dull the vigilance of their readers. If the son of peasants can study and become a lawyer, that means things aren't really so bad. I won't provide any services to those I should be fighting!"

"But you're a special case," I insisted.

"The special case serves as proof that anyone can make it— that's the only dialectic the class enemy is willing to accept!"

I didn't remember anything about this exchange during one of our meetings after the July 14th revolution. He had been released from the desert prison in Nuqrat al-Salman and after only a few weeks was appointed spokesman for the Ministry of Information, a position tailor made for him, and he threw all his analytic and rhetorical talents into it. Iraq then faced a dual confrontation from members of the Baghdad Pact who had given up the ghost on one hand and, on the other, from the champions of unity joining forces under the leadership of Abed al-Nasser. But what most worried the leaders of the revolution was the collapse of the agricultural economy following the mass exodus from the villages into the cities. The agricultural reforms, meant to better the lives of the peasants, ran headlong into the shameful phenomenon of sabotage perpetrated against the new Soviet tractors and combines, the abandonment of the villages and the squandering of generously donated funds on wanton mayhem and revelry at the local taverns and brothels. The peasants weren't to blame, Qassem told me, the blame should be laid on those who claimed for hundreds of years that the land was the cause of their servitude, until it penetrated deep into their consciousness, so the minute they felt free they fled towards the vain enchantments of the city. Analysis at its very best, not simply for the sake of righting injustice but to serve an ideology that is always just. I should have reminded him of the conversation we had more than twenty-five years ago and asked him why he still put all the blame on the class enemy without seeking any faults in the rash, makeshift proceedings of the agricultural reforms themselves. I'm sure that even to this, he would have found, as usual, an apologetic answer that perfectly hit the mark.

He sat in the nerve center of the new regime, as one of the prime intermediaries of the government, pronouncing declarations, briefing the press, raising the achievements of the revolution to miraculous levels, and fending off attacks from Cairo and Amman, Damascus and Teheran. He was at the height of his success, his demeanor on television was serious, acutely formulating his brilliant adages. But this success wouldn't last long—after Abed al-Salem 'Aref's opposition revolt, he was relieved of his position and could only expect imprisonment. He disappeared again and no one knew where he was hiding until he was caught at the border between Iran and the Soviet Union, along with a small group of persecuted Ba'athists. He fell into the hands of the *Savak* like easy prey, and they took their revenge brutally for the tongue lashing he had given the Shah's tyrannical regime. They pulled out his fingernails and broke his ribs and limbs before hanging him upside down and scalding his afflicted body with red hot stakes. After they brought him back to Iraq, in accordance with a pact initiating neighborly relations and friendship between the two countries, he limped along on one leg following the unsuccessful treatment he'd gotten for his other broken limb. These days the Iranians are accusing the Ba'ath regime of collaborating with *Savak*, and I just have to ask myself: isn't Qassem's crippled leg proof enough? From the *Savak* he was handed over to the *Mukhabarat*—the *Savak* tortured him because he was a communist who expressed animosity towards the Shah, and the *Mukhabarat* tortured him because he was a communist who opposed Ba'athist ideology. What does he think about all this now, in his exile? What kind of gruesome dreams inhabit his nights?

"We've been expelled from the garden of Eden," he told me once, "so it's up to us to build the garden of Eden ourselves, on this earth." Then he told me about al-Hallaj's book *al-Tawwaseen*, and how it fell into his hands while he was in prison. There he found a description of Satan that matched the very description of the fearless fighter. Among all the ministering angels, Satan alone refused to bow to Adam, so he was punished and expelled, knowing that if he obeyed the divine commandment, he would have no choice but to obey every other command, embarking on a never ending and vicious circle of submission. "Satan's insubordination is the very example that every fighter bearing the miracle of rebellion should take to heart," he said, "the Satan of the Quran is Prometheus, he is the rebel and not the ludicrous fool from the fairy tales about the garden of Eden!"

Qassem withstood the test of the first circle without submitting. Whenever he was asked about it, he would adopt a laconic tone and describe in detail the torture methods and the monstrous character of his interrogators without ever saying a word about himself. I guess it was easier to talk about the torments of the body than face the humiliation that must have hounded him like a nightmare. He covered up his pain with a thick skin, but sometimes he had a bewildered look about him, as if he were staring into the abyss.

He was sentenced to life after being handed over to the *Mukhabarat* and sent to Nuqrat al-Salman, that same infamous prison he was in during the monarchy. His trial was held behind closed doors, without the benefit of any defense and with no witnesses. Only his name appeared in a headline, saying the hand of justice had clamped down on one of the state's most dangerous enemies. After two years had gone by he was transferred to the central prison in the Hila district where most of the communists and those opposing the Ba'ath party were held. It was only there that Badriya could see him and hear the details of his escape to Iran. He had crossed the border through palm thickets near Basra where he was wounded in the shoulder by a border guard. But he managed to slip out of custody and, after a long trek through the night, he got to the Arab settlements near Awaz. He hid out there for a month, and with the help of members of the communist underground, he made it to Teheran and from there to the border between Iran and the Soviet Union.

It was an odd twist of fate for him to end up in prison in al-Hila, his birthplace, the last station on his afflicted way. In 1967, just before the war that brought disgrace upon the Arab world, he took his freedom, through a tunnel dug beneath two stone walls by prisoners with spoons and kitchen knives, leading out to a parking lot in a garage opposite the prison. This was the biggest prison break of its kind and it sent shock waves through the regime's hierarchy. The police and the army opened a wide dragnet to find the prisoners, but without much success. Just a year later, after the revolt of al-Bakr and his right hand man Sadaam Hussein, amnesty was declared for all the escaped prisoners and most of the detained communists.

Only a week after the escape, Qassem showed up at my house. It was around dusk on a cold and clear winter day and I was out moving the car from its parking space to the front gate when I saw a man in Arab dress, adorned with a white beard, holding a walking stick and leaning on the gate. I didn't recognize him until he stood by the gate and winked. I started trembling at the shock of seeing him and I felt like opening the gate and taking him in my arms. "Is the driver here?" was his first question. I thought he wanted to be taken somewhere, but then I realized he just wanted to know if there were any strangers in the house. I told him that the driver never stayed this late and only Hamida and the maid were around, and the maid was trustworthy. I brought him into the house and Hamida, seeing me come in with a guest, gave me a startled look and hurriedly withdrew into another room. "Umm Butheina," he called out in a hoarse, smitten voice. "Don't you want to greet me?" Stunned, she turned to him, her hand on her heart. "It's Qassem," I said, but she just stood there for a long moment, staring and mumbling: "Thank God, thank God!"

He walked right through the front door in the light of day like a distinguished sheikh coming for a visit, not a frightened fugitive with tattered clothes, scaling fences in the darkness of night like in the movies. That was Qassem, a dignified man who commanded respect. But beyond this exterior, the signs of suffering were evident—his face was gaunt and the hand clutching the walking stick was shaky. He hadn't ventured outside the perimeters of al-Hila the whole week, hiding out amongst old friends, making contact with members of the underground, and getting hold of some decent clothes and false documents. He got to Baghdad in a private car that he drove right to the corner. "I hope I haven't gotten you into any trouble," he told me. "You're a precious guest in this house and I am at your service," I replied. I said it in all sincerity, yet I couldn't help but remain astonished that he had chosen to come to my house, despite all the risks involved. But my astonishment faded quickly as Hamida went out with the maid to prepare some food. "I want to see Zuhair," he told me.

It wasn't refuge that he sought in my house, but a place he could meet Zuhair. I was confounded by his request, but reconciled myself to do everything he asked me for. I told Hamida that I was going out, without telling her where. I drove straight to Badriya's. I didn't even have time to think, although I was well aware the house was being watched and my arrival by car at such an hour was sure to arouse suspicion. But I was determined to do whatever I could for my childhood friend. Badriya was surprised to see me at the entrance and understood immediately that something must have happened. I tried to let her know there was nothing to worry about, and the only thing I said aloud was that they were invited over to our house for dinner that evening. She didn't say a word, and when Zuhair came out of his room wondering about this unexpected visit, I put my finger over my mouth signaling him not to ask any questions. Then I said it had been a while since they'd come over and that I had gotten a letter from Butheina in London asking after Zuhair and wondering why he hadn't written to her for such a long time. Everything I said was true, although it also justified my coming to get them, something I had never done before.

We were witnesses, Hamida and I, to their emotional reunion. Tears welled up in Qassem's eyes, but he tried to maintain his composure and even joke about the might of the prison guards. And when they sat at the table with him at the head and Zuhair by his side, I couldn't help but think to myself: here is a sixty-three year old man sitting at the dinner table with his family—such an ordinary thing, but so unimaginable.

He stayed over for one night. The next day, when I came back from work, he was already gone.

There it is—I've told a story better suited to silence. I'll try to concentrate on the past, but writing drags me into the present. Even so, I find it difficult to lay bare everything that's accumulated in my heart. I'm accustomed to concealing my thoughts, to keep up appearances, I'm just like everyone else close to the regime, ingratiating themselves to the despot, while turning a blind eye to his crimes.

I CAN'T REMEMBER IF it was in 1942 or 43 that I visited Qassem in his office, not far from City Hall, to give him a book about the Nestorian church. A few days earlier he had sat with us at the Zahawi cafe. We talked of the news, and the advance of the war, as well as the growing influence of the Communist party, especially after the German attack on Russia. Qassem, as usual, strongly rejected any criticism of Stalin, and praised his genius as a leader, that he could foil the British plot with its allies to encourage Hitler to destroy the Soviet Union. He refused, just as stubbornly, to see any connection between the Eastern front against Hitler and the Party's growing power in Iraq, although he had to admit the Party did benefit from the relative freedom in the country. "It's an imperialist tactic," he said. "Britain wants to gather support for the war against Hitler, but the people knows imperialists don't change their skin, lax today, furious tomorrow!" The Russians' bravery in defense of their homeland inspires every real patriot, he said, but what drives people to act is the understanding that only a new kind of party, communist and not social-democratic, is a guarantee for the people's victory in its struggle for independence, and the worker's victory over their exploiters. Turning to me, he did not forget to mention his Jewish comrades. "I'm full of admiration for the Jews," he said. "They serve as a model for every patriot who didn't experience what they went through during the *farhud*."

Kazem saw this as an opportunity to recount his experience during the two days of the *farhud*, when he stood at the gateway to the Fadhl neighborhood and stopped the rioters from hurting his Jewish neighbors. "Preventing a crime doesn't relieve responsibility for the crime," Qassem defied him.

"You accuse me of being responsible?" Kazem was astounded.

"Not you alone, I accuse all of us," he replied. "What did we do during the massacre of the Assyrians? Did we learn a lesson? On the contrary, we held triumphant parades for Bakr Sidqi as a national hero!"

"He was sent to put down a dangerous uprising," Kazem objected.

"It wasn't an uprising, it was cold blooded murder, the genocide of a helpless population. His soldiers massacred the frightened masses, raped women and slaughtered them, tore babies out of their mothers' arms and threw them in the river. It was a barbaric act, but we let it pass in silence, and everyone tried to ignore and forget the Nazi propaganda!"

Kazem was about to reply, but someone asked if the Assyrians are Armenian and he told him they were not Armenian but Turkish. I had to correct him and explain they belonged to the Nestorian church, whose center is in Turkey. As some of those present asked to learn more, I added some details on the history of this church that particularly aroused Qassem's curiosity. We didn't go back to discussing politics and Qassem moved to another table. Two or three days later he called me at the office and asked if I had some reading material about the Assyrians. I told him I had a book about the Nestorian church, not about contemporary Assyrians, and that I could lend it to him.

The next day I went to his office. A violent sandstorm blew that day. Strong winds had been blowing since the morning and toward noon, after the wind died down, a thick veil of brown dust that sticks to the clothes, the eyes, and mixes in with every breath, descended upon the city. Nothing better can be done on such a day than to shut the windows and block every hole in the house, indeed I was going to tell Qassem I wouldn't be coming to the cafe, but he was the first to call, to ask if I had brought the book, and suggested I come to his office. "Not a speck of dust here," he said. I found him sitting with a man of medium height, with a long meager face, who blinked with his tiny eyes as though he was near-sighted. "Meet comrade Fahed," he said, and the man stood up to shake my hand.

My astonishment was so obvious that Qassem burst out laughing: "Don't worry, we're not trying to recruit you into the party!"

I learned that Fahed wanted the book, after Qassem told him of our conversation in the cafe. I sat with them for a quarter of an hour or so and I have no recollection of what we said; we probably talked about the contents of the book which, by the way, was never returned to me. I was so impressed by this surprise meeting with the mystery man, the Communist Party's venerable leader; the security services had been trying to catch him for years. There was nothing conspicuous about him, except his tiny brown eyes, narrowed to thin slits when he spoke. But he didn't speak much, just chain-smoked.

I met Fahed again two months later. I was heading for one of the construction sites in the Jadid Hassan Pasha neighborhood when he passed by me, and had he not raised his hand a bit to greet me, I wouldn't have noticed him. He quickly slipped away and disappeared among the alleys. This encounter amazed me no less than the first, and when I asked Qassem if the man usually went out on his own in full daylight, he proudly replied: "They don't dare touch him, he's the most important man in Iraq today." Perhaps he was right, even though he had a tendency to exaggerate. In days to come, though, they were to lay their hands on him, and march him to the gallows.

DURING THE WAR YEARS I would meet Qassem every now and then and get news of Assad; he had turned to business in those days, and established an up to date printing and publishing enterprise. I tended to agree with Qassem about the young Jews who, unlike their parents, understood that the lesson of the *farhud* led to only one conclusion: the need to join the national struggle, not withdraw into the confines of the community. Nevertheless, I thought he overestimated the significance of this trend, especially since Zionist propaganda had begun to find supporters among them.

One day he approached me in jest: "It's time you face reality and admit your mistake."

"Admit what?" I asked.

"That you presented a biased vision."

"I wrote of what I know from the inside."

"I know Jews from the inside too, I live with them. They're great patriots."

"Precisely what I had wished for, that they be patriots."

"Don't try to wriggle out of it," he warned me. "You couldn't find a good word to write about them, and it's time you replied to the fascist instigators, tell them the Jews have withstood the toughest trial, and proven their loyalty to the homeland."

"The real test is Palestine," I replied.

"Palestine? You want them to go to Palestine to fight? Who sold Palestine to the Zionists? They're fighting for Iraq, we all fight for Iraq!"

"For Communism!"

"And that's the solution for all of us, for Palestine as well!"

The communists didn't like to discuss Palestine. When pressed, they'd direct their attack against the British, and the Arab rulers who followed them. They condemned Zionism as a nationalist ideology, but ignored its colonialist nature and failed to appreciate its actual power. Qassem believed that driving the British out of the region would lead to the collapse of existing regimes and pave the road for the rise of the Left. I remember, following the resolution to partition Palestine and the end of the British mandate, how he told me, almost celebrating: "Palestine is going to be the first country in the Middle East to be liberated from British rule!"

He was a man of faith and his faith gave him the power to persevere and withstand torture. But as a believer he sometimes made a mountain out of a molehill. As for myself, I observed the flow of Jews into the ranks of the Communist Party and other parties of the Left with great skepticism. Not that there was anything extraordinary about it; it only supported what I had written about Jews in the European Left, when I compared their status to that of Christians in the nationalist movements in Egypt and Syria. But all that remained on the surface for, as I said to Qassem, the real test was Palestine. Maybe, if it wasn't for Palestine, the Jews could have played a role similar to the Christians, but one can not use this hypothesis to come to conclusions about Judaism as a separatist world view.

Officially, Qassem was a member of al-Chadarchi's party; he gave speeches at party gatherings and published articles in *al-Ahali*, but everyone knew he was a communist, one of several communist activists, some of them Jewish, who worked inside the party in order to draw it further to the left. Al-Chadarchi didn't stop them, because he appreciated their capabilities, and he himself vacillated between Socialism of the Soviet type and that of the British Labour Party. Either way, al-Chadarchi knew how to use them to enhance public support for his party. I read *al-Ahali* every day and identified with the party's mainstream line, whose foremost representative was al-Chadarchi. But I refused to join the party, not only because I was a civil servant, but mainly due to my general disinclination to take on a binding commitment. I had several arguments with Qassem on this issue, and once he told me: "I know what stops you from joining, and I wouldn't be surprised if you joined the Istiqlal party, where you won't find any Jews!" I didn't join Istiqlal, and thank god I was wise enough to retire from Saleh Jabr's group in time. I kept my honor.

The ways of politics are tangled and I have no intention to mar these pages describing that period. I write of Qassem, the man who believed that victory was within reach. He was full of optimism in 1948, exciting the masses in the great demonstrations as one of the most popular speakers in the *wathba*, the big uprising that actually threatened the government. But even back then the communist leaders were already underground and, a year later, in February 1949, Fahed was hanged with two of his comrades. War in Palestine provided Nuri Sa'id and his gang an opportunity to settle accounts with their adversaries, and the hunt for communists was fully unleashed. Qassem was sentenced to life and sent to Nuqrat al-Salman.

I saw him in August 1958. He had just been released from prison and put in the Ministry of Information. He remained energetic and quick to respond but the years in prison had left their mark. His hair turned white and two wrinkles were arched deep in his cheeks on either side of his mouth. His vision was impaired by too much reading with too little light, and he began to wear glasses. He was full of optimism again, and this time I could only share his feeling, I too thought that a new era had begun. But when he told me, "They'll come back over time," I laughed. He was talking of the Jews who were, in his view, forced to emigrate. "We'll call upon them to return, Iraq is their homeland, and here is where they must be to participate in the building of the republic!" He told me of his Jewish comrades who were taken by force directly from prison to the airplanes, and sent to Israel against their will. He believed that pressure could be applied to the Zionist state to give up the cheap labor force and cannon fodder for their wars with the Arabs. How naive he was!

It wasn't the right time to argue with him, and I had just come back from the United States in a dismal state of mind. As the revolution broke out I stood by Jane's grave, and cried. I buried my youth there, my best years; I buried Haroun Saussan whom she had loved and wouldn't exchange for Ahmad. Her blunt words came back to me as Jamil and Butheina held me on either side, the Jew's son and the Muslim's daughter, my children. In those moments, plunging into the abyss, losing any sense of reality as my consciousness blurred, the words of the *kadish* and the *fatiha* leapt to my mind while I stared at a cross stuck into a mound of earth. What am I? Who am I?

It was in this introverted state of estrangement that I got news about the revolution. Suddenly the phone began ringing and I was asked to answer questions, to provide explanations, to analyze. The embassy people, in their distress, shut the gates to journalists, but one of the workers who knew where I was gave them my phone number. What answers could I offer? What did I know of the revolutionary leaders? What could I say about 'Abd al-Karim Qassem? I'd never heard his name. And I had no idea about factions in the army and secret negotiations with the communists and the Left. I did my job as the head of a government bureau, I edited the engineers' union newsletter, I was a member of the Academy of the Arab Language, and dedicated my evenings to reading and writing. I was outside of the events, in the margins, indeed, I am a marginal man.

I write of Qassem, of the man he always was inside, the warrior who never aspired for position or status but used his position and status to serve the redemptive ideals in which he believed, to serve the people, his origins, to serve the peasant he didn't want to be. After being relieved of his position, he headed south, to the bilharzia infested marshlands in al-Gharraf, in the Kut district, to the wretched of the earth, the rice growers who put guard dogs out at night to protect them from the jackals that bit the rotten flesh of their feet. Among these god-forsaken people he stood as a leader, calling for revolt, reviving dead souls. Qassem is the man of whom epic poems are written, he was molded from the good soil and the waters of the Euphrates, of the race of mythic heroes, the descendants of Adonis and Gilgamesh!

I saw him in the winter of 1968, after amnesty for the Hila prison escapees was declared. He looked ten years older, though only a year had passed since he showed up at my house. The communists were back in the game after 'Aref's demise and after al-Bakr and Sadaam Hussein took power. Qassem's permit to practice law was reinstated and he opened a partnership with Aziz Laham who had done his appreticeship with Qassem in the forties. It looked as though at last he was going to find some rest and allow younger people to do the work, but a man like him couldn't quit the struggle and, when the disagreement with the Ba'ath leadership emerged, he was one of the leaders to divide the party into those opposing and those supporting participation in the government. A violent conflict took place among the communists and some say he was among the planners of a series of assassinations of Ba'ath collaborators. I will never know the truth, because he went underground again, and finally fled.

Aziz Laham was caught and gave a much talked of testimony about a communist conspiracy to overthrow the revolutionary government. That detestable scoundrel's conscience didn't stop him from slandering his own instructor and leader. Now I hear he is going to be made Cultural Attaché at the embassy in Paris. No less. A traitor and a drunkard will represent us in cultural institutions, and Qassem is in exile!

THREE YEARS AFTER QASSEM found refuge in Czechoslovakia, Assad fled to Israel. I'll probably never see either of them again. I've just listened to Assad's voice once more, on the cassette, and wonder if he'll mention me when he completes his memoirs. I think of this with mixed feelings. Curiosity moves me to wonder how he would describe me and present our relationship, at the same time I wish he wouldn't violate the truce of friendship and make public the disagreement that tore us apart. As loyal Hilawis we both kept silent, and if I violate the truce in these pages I do so knowing that my words won't see the light of day during our lifetime. I write for the generations to come, for the children of the next millennium, when these pages will no longer count, in the government's eyes, as an indictment, and our lives and deeds will belong to history.

After the *farhud* I didn't initiate a meeting with Assad, nor did I invite him to my wedding. I didn't want him to turn me down and, even more than that, I didn't want to make him feel uneasy were he to accept the invitation. My own discomfort at marrying a young woman, almost against my will, was enough. Assad had become the owner of a printing operation, and in the days to come he would establish a press that became the destination for young poets. His printing plant was one of the most advanced for the time, and his affairs expanded and flourished, especially as commercial firms and government institutions began to regularly take their printing jobs to him. Kazem was among those who approached him to print ads and contracts for the grain trading company he was a partner in, and through him, as well as through Qassem until he was arrested, I would send him regards just as he sent them to me. We never actually met; in fact, there was no reason for us to meet, we had parted ways and both of us preferred to leave things as they were without making any pronouncements.

Of all times, it was in 1951, the year of mass Jewish emigration, that we happened to make contact. The National Lands Administration I headed then had prepared a large survey on the legal status of agricultural parcels in the northern region and up to date information was sent to the government press, where we usually sent our administrative documents for publication. But after a four month wait we were told that due to a work overload the printer wouldn't be able to stand by their obligation to us. We had to find another printer, and the only solution we could come up with was passing the material on to Assad's firm. I asked the secretary to go over everything with him, and he agreed to do the job. Then the unexpected happened. There was a technical problem with the tables of weights and prices which, for some reason, the secretary couldn't straighten out with Assad. Without even asking, the phone was passed on to me. We were both a little confused for a second, finding ourselves on two ends of a phone line, a printer and his customer, after so many years of severed relations. We exchanged polite greetings and solved the problem but I couldn't just end the conversation as if it were only business. I asked him how he felt in light of the new situation. "You can't really expect good tidings from me," he answered. I told him that I always hoped to hear of good things from him. "There aren't any good things these days. We live in the midst of a whirlpool and no one knows where it will take us." I told him that maybe it was for the better, whoever goes goes, and whoever stays could at least maintain their dignity. He responded with bitterness: "If dignity means holding an affidavit preserving your citizenship, then that's a pretty fishy kind of dignity, as good as a yellow badge."

I saw no point in replying, and ended the conversation with some pat phrase. He spoke in distress, and who but I could understand what he must have been going through. But the analogy was out of place. It wasn't because of discrimination that those remaining were asked to carry the certificate, just the opposite, it was in order to preserve their rights in the enormous confusion that was created when thousands of Jews who renounced their citizenship and were, in effect, bereft of any legal status, continued conducting their business as usual, right up until it was their turn to board a plane heading out.

When I told Kazem what we had talked about, he looked at his prayer beads for a while before saying: "If I was in his place, I wouldn't stay."

I was flabbergasted by his response, even though I had heard him speak of the émigrés with sympathy more than once. "You would suggest that Assad emigrate to Israel?" I asked.

"I didn't say I would suggest he emigrate. I said, if I were in his place. I don't foresee life being easy for those who stay."

Nor did I expect life to be easy for the few thousand who chose to stay. Most of them were property owners, merchants, functionaries in civic institutions, or senior civil servants who were made to retire. But to think of someone like Assad Nissim getting up and joining this crowd, to show him the way out, something like that just seemed contrary to any kind of logic. As I drove by on my way from al-Sa'adun Avenue, I would stop occasionally by the sidewalk opposite the Massouda Shemtob Synagogue and stare at the noisy crowds assembled at the gate. Israeli agents got what they wanted when they planted bombs in the synagogues, for they managed to sow panic among Jews who hadn't exactly rushed to sign on for immigration at first. They worked hand in hand with the authorities to realize the Zionist program, and Jewish money worked on the decision makers who had made a covenant with the enemy. Looking at those Jews, my heart sank thinking of my sisters and the rest of the family, probably standing among them. I didn't worry about the immigrants, I even felt sort of smug that they were pulling out; yet, it was impossible to remain indifferent to their wretched appearance, the miserable future awaiting them, their being used as pawns in a game between Zionist emissaries and avaricious government ministers. Just then I was told of the jolting speech given by the Jewish dignitary Ezra Daniel in a closed session of the Senate. I had known him when I was a child because my father was responsible for his family's property in al-Hila; if my memory serves me well, he died of a stroke just a year after this. He was a member of the Senate and one of the most prominent of the Jewish dignitaries who not only remained unsympathetic to the Zionists but even condemned them at different times. His speech at that session wasn't published because it included details incriminating the government, particularly Nuri Sa'id who, already in the twenties, had given the Zionist emissaries free reign despite opposition by the leadership of the community.

Assad stayed on and continued to run the press and the printing operation. In 1956 he published a collection of his poetry, making sure that a copy was sent to me. I called to congratulate and thank him, and he invited me to a party at the offices of the press, right next to his house in the Masbah Quarter. One of the editors of *al-Hawdeth* whose name escapes me, gave quite a comprehensive lecture on Assad's poetic path, as well as on his other literary activities. Then Assad read some poems from the new book. A younger poet also spoke—he formed part of a group of younger poets who found a home for their work at Assad's press. He spared no praises for Assad's support and high standards, but said nothing about his poetry. I told Kazem, sitting next to me, that the younger people valued Assad as a person, but didn't think much of his poetry. He nodded in agreement. The newer poetry didn't really move him, nor did it move me; we remained hostages to the magic of rhyme and meter and the innovations of younger poets who rebelled against meter and rhyme alienated us. Assad belonged to a generation whose time had passed, and only the great al-Jawahiri continues to raise the honorable standard of the wounded poetry.

It turned out that this event was to be Assad's farewell party. I didn't get another chance to see him, and as the years went on it became harder to renew our ties. I kept up with his writing in the papers, and found his name among the communal leaders who congratulated Abed al-Karim Qassem after the revolution, and congratulated him again after he survived an attempt on his life. Afterwards, they congratulated Abed al-Salam 'Aref who murdered Abed al-Karim Qassem and took his place. After the death of that one, they congratulated his brother, chosen as president. And then al-Bakr who followed him. He continued to fulfill his function, and he continued to pay the price for cleaving to his Jewishness. The situation got worse for Jews under 'Aref's regime, and Assad, along with the chief rabbi and a handful of dignitaries, brought their complaints to the authorities.

I still have the speech that Assad delivered before Abed al-Rahman 'Aref who took his brother's place after the latter perished in a plane crash. The speech he delivered in the meeting between communal leaders and the President was published in full in the papers, on the explicit orders of 'Aref himself since he had found it so impressive. "I who grew up on the banks of the Tigris and the Euphrates, who sang the love of my homeland and who dedicated the greater part of my life to the benefit of native art, do I deserve to be humiliated, abused and left bereft of any rights? Isn't it tragic that a man like myself could be considered disloyal to his homeland just because he is a Jew?"

Those were his words, and I quote them word for word. Indeed, his situation was tragic, in the classical meaning of the word. He made a mistake when he chose to stick to Judaism, and another, as Kazem had predicted, when he chose to stay in Iraq. But this was Assad, a divided soul. He adapted to his situation, and went on seeking appointments with presidents and government ministers, kept dispatching letters and asking for justice for his disappearing community. The curtain went down on Assad the poet and no one remembered him until someone saw fit to use him in a sophisticated propaganda campaign, appoint him to the Arab Writers Conference and shower him with praise. Even then he fulfilled his function, reading out his poems, participating in literary events, and appearing on television shows. I saw and heard and wondered. What was happening in his heart? Was he as satisfied as he made sure to appear?

TODAY I'M BACK AT my desk, not having touched these pages in more than a month. First I was distracted by Sabry's trip, then I experienced intense back pain and was ordered to lie down for two entire weeks. Due to the tension with Iran, the Interior Ministry has imposed severe limitations on exit visa applications and Sabry, who had lingered for so long before finally deciding to go, was met with rejection. I had to employ anyone who could move anything to get him the visa, and at long last had no choice but to approach Maulud Tikriti. The morning after he left I was unable to get up and the doctor ordered me to lie on a hard bed. Hamida sat next to me most of the day and wouldn't let me read; when Sarah came back from kindergarten, the bedroom became a play room: toy-blocks and dolls, bears and elephants, a fire engine with a loud whistle and a train bustling along its winding tracks. Sarah is Hamida's great joy, and the focus of her worries. She sings to her, tosses her in her lap and plays with her, and suddenly a cloud comes over her face and she mumbles: "Poor thing, she'll grow up without a father."

She gloomily accepted the news of Sabry's departure, not saying a word while we ran around to get his visa. In her heart she was hoping they wouldn't let him out. Butheina was under immense pressure and didn't feel relieved of it even after the visa was granted, fearing he might change his mind. "I know him," she told me, stiffly leaning her head in the way she had inherited from Reuben. "He's childish, and might just waive his visa to play the hero who tricked everyone!" But Sabry didn't play the hero and didn't intend to trick anyone, he went because he realized he had to go. He left with a heavy heart. Takriti himself told me: "Tell him to get out quickly." I avoided asking for his help after he turned me down about Zuhair, but when I saw how nothing budged, and time was passing, I visited his office and he resolved the problem with a phone call. Sabry's file had already been passed on to the *Mukhabarat*, and had he not gotten out in time his situation would have been very serious. I gave him gifts for Jamil and the children, and accompanied him to the airport together with his parents, lest there be some last minute delay.

That night my back hurt, and the next morning I couldn't get out of bed. Hamida was quick to call Dr. Hikmat, and so I spent two stupefying weeks on my back, having empty conversations with Hamida. "You worry for Sarah, and I worry for Butheina," I told her over and over, for lack of another topic to discuss with her. And she replied: "Only you worry? Can we tell who she'd end up with? And how he'll treat the girl? Today's men, you can't trust them." And I'd say: "Butheina is still young and we have to help her rebuild her life." And she: "And what do I do? Who takes care of the girl?" And I: "Sabry is an excellent fellow, but they weren't a good match." And she: "If you had talked to her, if you'd taken care of her the way a father takes care of his daughter, they wouldn't have separated." And I: "Butheina is a serious young woman, and Sabry is a bit frivolous." And she: "The fingers of one hand are not all the same. Haven't I suffered? Do you pay attention to me? Spending all your time with your books! But a woman has to accept what god allots her!"

These were our conversations, and when we fell silent I would ask myself: Do I have anything to complain about? Hamida, in spite of her grumbling, let me pursue what was close to my heart and never posed any conditions I couldn't withstand. Thirty five years without matching, perhaps even without love. Jane was love, but I never made up with Jane. Maybe that was the key to marriage? Mutual acceptance, like the fingers of a hand, all connected and each on its own? Hamida never forgets to nag me for not carrying out my fatherly duty to prevent the divorce, at least for the girl's sake. And when anger overtakes her she really lets me have it: "What else can you expect from a man who deserted his son?" She knows my weak spot, and it leaves me speechless. In our confrontations, she always has the last word.

Butheina's personality isn't like her mother's, but she bears a grudge just like her. "I have an orphan brother," she wept. She hadn't forgiven me, ever since that incident at school, ever since she learned that she had a brother in America and that I had hidden my past from her. She concealed her anger for years, and once she met her brother by his mother's grave she lashed out at me. In her eyes I was guilty of making Jamil an orphan even before he lost his mother. She was thirteen and I assumed this outburst had released her distress, staying in touch with her brother would remove the remains of this grudge. I was mistaken. And I realized my mistake at the hospital in Poitier, where she studied. We came to be near her when she gave birth, and Hamida dragged me out on daily shopping trips, for a crib, for a stroller, for all the required equipment. She also arranged one of the two bedrooms for the baby, according to her taste, and sewed, with her own hands, little pouches with scrolls of blessing against the evil eye that she had procured before we left. She never gave up on such matters, and there was no point resisting her.

Butheina gave birth late at night and Sabry broke the news to us over the phone. We saw her the next day, all smiles with the baby at her side. "She wants to name her Sarah," Sabry said. "Yes," Butheina confirmed, looking at me. Hamida, taking the baby in her arms, was full of joy, as if she hadn't heard, but when we left the room she turned to Sabry: "And you agree?" Sabry shrugged his shoulders and looked at me. Hamida also gave me a reproachful look. I said nothing, and we remained silent in the corridor.

"She's taking her revenge on you," Hamida told me later. And added: "She wants it known that the girl's grandfather is Jewish. She hasn't forgotten what she had to go through because of you!"

I never replied to all this, and never asked Butheina. And yet, whenever I heard her explain to people, almost apologetically, "It's a pretty name," my heart sank.

I'LL HAVE TO PUT aside, so it seems, these pages of memoirs and all my other engagements. I got the the final manuscript of the translation and, for two days, have been toiling on the first chapter alone. Errors and inaccuracies abound in almost every line. Just the thought of having to go through more than eight-hundred dense pages makes me shudder. Butheina promised to help me, but she has precious little free time of her own. I relish her company; she's calm and finds great satisfaction in her work at the university. She's an excellent teacher, but has a long way ahead of her to prove herself in research.

Hamida has gone back to the photo albums. "Daddy in America with Uncle Jamil," she tells Sarah. "He'll bring you lots of presents. What do you want him to give you? An American doll? No. He'll give you a pretty dress. A bride's dress! All the girls will envy you: Look how pretty Sarah is, her father came back from America and he loves her!" That's how she talks to her now. No longer claiming that Sarah is angry at her father, and turning the page when she sees his picture. May she never take up the old tune again, bu with Hamida there's no telling, everything can turn.

RELATIONS WITH IRAN ARE getting complicated. The papers are calling for Iranian subjects to be put in internment camps. The fifth column must be weeded out, the headlines cry. This reminds me of the headlines twelve years ago. The fifth column was the handful of Jews still in Iraq; then too the proposal was to put them in an internment camp in Rashidiya, next to the psychiatric hospital. But things are different now, for then we had no one to fight. Israel struck a hard blow, and the whole world was amazed by the Jewish army's crushing power. Now calls for revenge on the Iranians foretell a real war, and I ask myself, are we really fit for war? A columnist in *al-Jumhuriya* warns that Israel won't sit back if a war breaks out, but his conclusion contradicts his warning as he stirs up his readers with the rhetoric of a war-monger: "The long border with Iran that stood for centuries like an impregnable wall against the Mongols and the Tatars will now withstand the new barbarism of Khomeini and his gang!" He adds: "The Iraqi people, and the entire Arab nation, look up to our brave soldiers, sentries by Arab culture's Eastern doorway who will mercilessly defeat the new barbarians, just as our ancestors under Salah al-Din defeated European barbarism!"

I beg for mercy on Kazem's soul, redeemed before having to witness a civil war that could break out at any moment. The Da'awa group's acts of terror increase every day, and the government reacts by carrying out mass arrests, and executing Shi'ites. Current events won't let me concentrate on writing my memoirs. It's hard to restrain yourself from crying out, if only on this piece of paper, against the despicable murder of twenty-one of the Ba'ath's best cadres. No one in his right mind would believe they conspired with the Iranian enemy or the Zionists. I ask: if we must ready ourselves for a threat from the East, who can guarantee we'll be able to meet a threat from the West? Anwar al-Sadat flew to Jerusalem and deserted the fateful battle with Zionism, while we talk of Islamic barbarism in the East and doing nothing against Zionist barbarism in the West. A war of Muslims against Muslims, Sunnis against Shi'ites, could Israel have hoped for anything better?

"We lack a Sakharov," Jawad al-'Alawi told me yesterday. I asked him: "Would he have been allowed to speak?" And he replied: "That's the reason you won't find a Sakharov among us."

And as if all these sad turns were not enough, now I hear that none other than Aziz Laham is handling Zuhair's case! Hamida found out from Badriya that Aziz saw Zuhair in prison and convinced him to confess to assisting a terrorist organization. Badriya pinned all her hopes on Aziz, Hamida says. He promised her that Zuhair would be indicted on a minor criminal count and there's a good chance he might even be released. What can one say about this? What a blow to Qassem! Zuhair admits to Islamist activity, anathema to him, and Aziz, who had betrayed him and his comrades, represents him! But what made Zuhair see him, and heed his counsel? And Badriya, it's as if she forgot the brutality with which he had informed on Qassem! Now I understand why he told me that Zuhair was a victim of my book. Perhaps he'll make him say that in court too. One can expect anything from this man.

Someone is overseeing all this. Someone sent him to Zuhair to use his trial as propaganda against subversive elements on the inside, and he'll gain yet another pat on the back for being a loyal patriot, and then get sent to represent us in Paris!

I thought that work on the translation would take most of my time and prevent me from continuing to write my memoirs. Now I find comfort in this work, it frees me from thinking about everything that's going on around me and provides me with yet more proof as to just how correct my conclusions were regarding Judaism and Islam.

BUTHEINA WON'T BE ABLE to go on helping me. She'll be off in two weeks to an international conference in Athens and has to prepare her lecture. This trip wasn't at all on the agenda, and she deliberated before giving the rector her approval. He told her the man that was supposed to go, a professor of economics from Basra University, couldn't attend, and the Ministry of Education suggested he send someone else. He never told her what prevented the man from attending, but just asked her to agree since attending this important conference, particularly in these times, could improve her position at the university. "I hate to replace the man who fell out of grace with them," she told me. "How will I answer when I'm asked why he couldn't come?" I told her: "You're going in your own right, and if someone is prevented from going on political grounds, that's not your fault."

I doubt that I won her over with this argument, but she realized it wouldn't be wise to refuse. Her lecture topic was a discussion of

Marseille's trade status with Middle Eastern ports in the eighteenth century. She'd worked on this subject in her dissertation, but for the last two years had been studying newly recovered documents. She lingers in the library now more than usual, sometimes only coming back after Sarah's dinner and bath. Hamida doesn't complain at all.

I MET MUNIR SARQIS in the Academy building. I told him it's where he should always be. He got my meaning and replied: "I'm used to working on my own." We're all individualists, I said, and that's just why we have to have an exchange of views with our colleagues. He laughed: "An exchange of views, yes, but I'm frustrated by the meetings."

I told him I was carefully checking the translation of *The Jews in History* and planned to add a preface, touching on more recent events. "That would be desirable," he said, "especially since it's getting published by the Ministry of Information." Regardless, I said, I saw a need to explain my views so as not to arouse confusion among foreign readers. He agreed again, and added: "Such explanation would, in fact, be needed for Arab readers too."

It was a valid comment, and I'm glad he volunteered it without my asking. He is a clever young man, and no one can better appreciate the delicacy of my current situation. Now I'm determined not to make do with a short explanation, but elaborately deliver my views on the issue of the conflict between Muslim civilization and Judeo-Christian civilization. It would be my credo in the face of fundamentalist Islam and Zionist aggression.

At the board meeting I proposed, in light of the new situation, a postponement of the fortieth anniversary celebrations, but Moustafa was firmly opposed and, to my surprise, everyone present sided with him, including Jawad. The idea came from the Minister and we can't call celebrations off by ourselves, they said. I wanted to get rid of a nuisance I didn't care for, but I failed. Maybe I'd find an opportunity to talk to the Minister about it. I'm sure he wouldn't object.

I decided to pay my debt to Munir Sarqis and suggested we invite him to join the General Council. I spoke highly of him, and said his contribution to the discussions would be significant. No one opposed me on this and Jawad added praise of Munir's special talents and linguistic sensitivities. But, as he is a civil servant, we must first have the approval of the Ministry of Information. Moustafa took it upon himself to see to that.

DREAMS DON'T COME TO us without being provoked externally, which is what happened to me yesterday when I woke up at five in the morning, precisely the hour I had intended to get up. I found myself on someone's trail and soon I saw Kazem and said something as I approached him, even though I was astonished that I could talk to him while he was no longer amongst the living; then I realized that it wasn't Kazem but my faithful servant Sha'aban and that I wanted him to come by and light the fire since the Sabbath had already begun, but he handed me something that I couldn't quite identify, a book or a sheaf of papers that turned into a distant inscription bearing strange and blurred letters, and I struggled to tell him that I couldn't read it, and he smiled at me strangely as he nodded his head. I was just on the verge of waking up when I went back and said to myself that Sha'aban too, after all, had been dead for a long time and he hadn't been in al-Hila and it couldn't have been him that I was looking for to come and light the fire.

The strands of this vision still bound me for some time as I was coming to and when I actually got up I decided to write it down before it fled from memory or became confused with all kinds of addenda that appear in the wake of the relentless machinations of consciousness. Clearly this dream was not unconnected to what I had been preoccupied with in those days, when I spent most of my time checking the translation, incessantly thinking over the preface that I had to write for the English edition. Laid before me now is Part Four, dealing with the Biblical narratives in light of archaeological discoveries. I had intended to get up early yesterday and finish checking it before the messenger came in the afternoon. But I didn't check the translation and, instead, found myself absorbed in reading a packet of my letters to Jane. This packet was kept in a file folder bound with a lace clasp and remained on the bottom shelf of the writing desk for some twenty years, from the day Jamil gave it to me on the visit he had paid us after his marriage. He came with Ursula, his wife, and we spent two happy weeks together. We went up North with them to the Kurdish parts and spent several days at Hotel Salah al-Din, at the foot of Mount Sifin; afterwards we went down to the site of ancient Babylon, toured al-Hila and cruised down in a sailboat right up to the entrance of Basra. "I took the liberty of peeking into the letters," Jamil told me as he was handing them over, "I knew of their existence, but I never dared to loosen the clasp until I moved into the new apartment. You wrote mother beautiful letters and I thought they should come back to you."

I found this gesture very moving—as happy as I was to get the letters back, I was even happier at the attention I got from Jamil. Nor did I dare to loosen the clasp on the packet—I hadn't touched them since the day I put them down on the bottom shelf of the desk. But life provides an odd amalgamation of events that sometime seem to act as if they were depicted by writers of cheap novels. In the evening

I sat with Hamida and Butheina after she put Sarah to bed and we all looked at a map of Athens together. I had already had the chance to visit that splendid city three times, and I was no less familiar with it than New York. I pointed out all the places worth visiting and suggested to Butheina that she skip going to the shops and make an effort to see everything that wasn't included on the round of tours prepared for those going to the conference. She said that she wouldn't feel comfortable walking around alone in an unknown city whose language she didn't even know, and here Hamida hastened to caution her about wandering around unaccompanied; she reminded her of the visit to London, when I waited for her at the entrance to the Underground station just a block away from the hotel and she, for some reason, strayed from the route even though we had gone the same way a number of times, ending up in a real panic. Although Butheina knew this story down to the minutest detail, she always asked her mother to tell it again, exaggerating more and more until she was brought to bursts of laughter. Meanwhile, I was also drawn in to tell the story of my going astray in the alley-ways of al-Hila, when I was four or five. My mother had sent me to deliver a message to a house that stood at the head of the neighborhood and I decided to go a little further, past the house, and suddenly I found myself in unfamiliar alleys with a gang of kids surrounding and harassing me. And as I was telling the story, I had a faint memory of having told of this incident once before but then I also described the fear I had as a Jew amongst the hostile Muslim kids. This fear, I must say, sometimes visits me in dreams.

We went back to speaking about Athens and the preparations for the trip, but I was already overtaken by anxiety over my inability to remember whom I had told the story of my getting lost to and whether or not I had told it all. It was only after we parted and

I went back to my room, while I was getting undressed and preparing to get into bed, that a spark went through my brain and I remembered the letters that I had sent to Jane.

A strange combination of events, attended by a disordered array of substance and delusion, discrete memories and astonishing revelations. If I hadn't told the story of my straying off in al-Hila, I wouldn't have remembered the letters to Jane, and if I hadn't remembered them before going to sleep maybe I wouldn't have dreamt the dream that left me in such great distress, and if it wasn't for the dream I doubt that I would have found the packet in its hiding place and gotten caught up in a reading that took me out of my world and brought me back to that of my lost youth. After all, isn't that the story of my life? A love story in letters, of what value is all the rest, the struggles, the disputes, the search for honor, the recognition? This is the story of Harry, as they used to call me and as I used to sign the letters, the story of the Jew who has passed from this world where only his spirit remains bound in this sheaf of a great love, sublime, hopeless. I read and I wept, I read and sunk to the abyss, I read and was surprised by the polished English whose perfection I can no longer achieve.

> I am standing at the banks of the Euphrates, gazing at the kids playing with smooth pebbles, listening to the fisherman's sweet song and in my heart the words of another song reverberate, an ancient song of praise that the Babylonians sang in their rituals of sacrifice to the holy river:
>
> O great and powerful river
> your beds were dug by the hand of gods
> river unlike any other

crowned in adoration and power
your shores are the gods' tabernacles
and your waters restore the soul
accept me with mercy
take from my body to nourish
the earth with abundance and blessings
take me, then, into your very depths. . .

YEARNING FOR LOVE AND yearning for the soil of his homeland, isn't the rending between these two loves the essence of Haroun Saussan's life? I found the letter in which I wrote of my going astray, dated 4.6.34, two months after Jane's departure. A four page letter describing the Jewish Quarter of al-Hila and the ways of its residents, with an abundance of illuminating details, long consigned to oblivion in my heart. Letters from that period and from the following years, arranged according to the date they were written, the first ones on the bottom and the last on top, recount at length the events that concerned me, my meetings with my sister Na'ima who brought me news from the family, the relations of the leaders of the community towards me, Reuben's attempts at reconciliation and Assad's efforts to support me. I also found letters from my first days in Baghdad, after my return from America, describing my work for the municipality, the house that I rented, my feelings of alienation in my country and amongst my friends, my reminding Jane of conversations and meetings, moments of sorrow and high spirits from our great days at the university. Six letters from the boat after my first visit collapse under the burden of philosophical reflections on self-consciousness, on freedom and solitude, on the human being who discovers he is bereft of roots and is nourished by sources in the air, like a plant torn out of the soil of its growth. A whole world is concealed in those letters, my world, a world that deserved to be brought into the pages of my memoirs instead of burrowing back into the depths of treacherous memory.

I didn't read the letters in order. Skipping some and lingering over others, I moved to and fro with the reins extended until I came upon a letter from the 7th of February, 1931, that astonished me. For a long moment I found myself gripped by a strange feeling, like someone who has undergone a mystical experience. It wasn't the contents of the letter that effected me but its connection to the dream I had dreamt, when I was asked to read an inscription and couldn't. In the first part of the letter I told of the heavy rains that had fallen on Baghdad, causing major flooding, and in the second part where I presented a comparison of the folktales of different peoples, apparently in answer to something in Jane's letter, I found the following lines:

> In the Quran we encounter many folktales whose sources can be found in the Hebrew Bible, but there is one particularly significant tale in the Book of Genesis which can be found in quite a different version in the Islamic tradition. This tale narrates the story of Jacob, who is Israel, and who encounters an angel of the Lord and wrestles with him the whole night without giving in. In the Islamic version we are told of Muhammad whose custom it was to seek seclusion in a cave near the city of Mecca. It was there that the angel Gabriel first discovered him and commanded unto him: "Read!" But Muhammad, who knew not how to read, answered: "I am unable to." The angel grasped him in a tight grasp until he was greatly pained only to, upon letting go, repeat his command: "Read!" His

breath cut off, Muhammad mumbled: "I am unable to." The angel grasped him again until it seemed to Muhammad that his spirit was about to flee from him, and when he was unhanded the angel again repeated his command: "Read!" Again Muhammad replied: "I am unable to." Then the angel moved away from him and taught him the first portions of the revelation: "Read in the name of your Lord who created /Created man from clotted blood /Read, for your Lord is the most beneficent / Who has taught by the pen / Taught man what he did not know."

The symbolism of these two versions is most illuminating. For while Jacob wrestles with the angel without submitting, Muhammad didn't even try to defend himself; thus can be found the difference between Islam, whose meaning is reconciliation and submission, and the children of Israel, stiff necked and ever rebellious against the Lord!

HOW CAN ONE EXPLAIN that which goes beyond logic? In the dream I was asked to read something and I couldn't. And here I am, at a story I noted down forty-nine years ago! The discovery agitated me and only after reconsidering things did I grasp that my unconscious had come to help me write the English preface that I had been preoccupied with for days. The story of the angel would serve as a point of departure through which I could explain not only the difference between Judaism and Islam, but also my own views on genuine Islam, that primal and pure Islam that came before power and disputes and division and bloodshed. Faith in the word and not the sword is the message that Muhammad bore at the beginning of his mission and it is this message that the Muslims of today must bear to their people and to the world. Only through the might of the word, which is wisdom and knowledge, can people find salvation from the despotism of rulers, from those lusting after power and from the ignorance of zealots addicted to malice.

The riddle of the dream was solved. I sense myself freed in a way I never had before. Aziz Laham carried out his threat. In an interview marking his appointment to a diplomatic mission, he found an opportunity to aim his darts at me. "It was with great interest that I read Dr. Ahmad Haroun Saussan's book," he said, "a serious book whose appearance must be congratulated, although it seems to me that his argument in favor of the Islamic revolution is liable to mislead, to turn honest readers into opponents who might interpret his claims as support for the Khomeini regime. I am also surprised that the author omitted his first book from the long list of his publications, *My Path to Islam*, which, to the best of my knowledge, was his first book in Arabic."

Thus, with the elegance of a future diplomat—and adding on my childhood name—did he cast the venom brewing in his twisted soul at me. But I no longer care about any of this. On the contrary, I find it preferable for my readers to know precisely from where I came, and whoever hasn't heard of the book can find it in the library and see for themselves that Ahmad Haroun Saussan has not strayed one single iota from what he wrote forty-five years ago. I am calm, as the proverb says: "If my slander issues from the mouth of a blemished man, does he not therefore serve witness to my remaining intact!"

I kept the paper away from Butheina's sight since I didn't want to worry her just as she was leaving, but she found out about the interview while talking to one of her friends on the phone and came back trembling. "Such things don't even deserve a response," I told her, "I have nothing to hide, but everyone knows who Aziz Laham is."

"But he's accusing you of supporting Khomeini!"

"Apparently that will be his line of defense when it comes to Zuhair."

"And you're keeping quiet?"

"If my book will lighten Zuhair's sentence, I'd be happy."

She was surprised by my resolve. I told her that Zuhair needed to be defended, that our youth needed to be defended, that Iraq needed to be defended, not me.

I accompanied her to the airport and on the way we spoke of Athens and all its beauty. She was calm as she departed from me and I could only hope that as she went up into the plane she had freed herself from worries about her father and begun to concentrate on what was awaiting her at the conference.

Afterwards I sat in the cafeteria and ordered tea with a piece of cake. Soldiers stood in every corner, suspiciously following the crowd as it moved here and there. A group of tourists, their faces tanned, bags strapped to their shoulders, wandered past the check-in counters. A mixture of dress, a mixture of races, and the announcer's voice thrashing in your ears. A way station. A border spot not on the border. A magnificent building that is nothing but a station, requiring only a ticket bearer and a name written on some passenger list. An airport is a kind of no-man's land, governed by people who can't be seen, turning numbers and letters on the board of arrivals and departures, announcing orders on high-powered loudspeakers, and the passengers glance furtively around themselves, standing in line and waiting, carrying their luggage and hastening their steps. A crowd in perpetual motion, and only the one sitting in the cafeteria and having tea with cake can take his time, feeling smug. He isn't traveling or rushing anywhere. He has exhausted his paths in life; having just now parted from his daughter, he will soon go back home where he will write the preface to the English edition and complete the book of memoirs that will never see the light of day during his lifetime.

(August '89–August '90)